A FAIRY TALE
KIND OF LOVE

Book One of the Lincks Series

Carol Clay

Published by Hear My Heart Publishing

ISBN: 978-0-9862331-3-5

A product of the United States of America.

Written by Carol Clay, carolclaywrites.com
Cover design by Jonna Feavel, 40daygraphics.com
Edited by Gene La Viness and Michelle Lehman

Dedication

This book is dedicated first to God for His blessing and His guidance.

To Raymond for his reassurance when I decided to do this.

To Jennifer for being my first "editor" and helping me to find the story in my words.

To Becky for her belief in me.

To Renee` and Critical Ink for their loving critique of my first book.

To Gene and Michelle for their editing.

To friends too numerous to mention, but you know who you are, for your support and encouragement.

And finally to Beth for taking a chance with me.

I thank you and love you all.

Chapter One

Danielle McMichaels had stopped only once to grab a hamburger from a fast food restaurant and feed Micah Jr. while she had been driving the interstate southwest from Chicago since noon. She never noticed the crystal clear afternoon sky of summer or the shimmer from the heat radiating from the asphalt. She did not see the rolling valleys or the hill country she was approaching. Her thoughts were only on what lay ahead, trying hard to forget what was behind her. The pain was too fresh to think about.

The nightmare of the last four months came back to her each time she allowed her mind to wander. She sought a happy memory, like the first time she scampered up the big oak tree to beat her brother to the top, but just as quickly, she relived the news of his death. Micah Lucas, her half-brother, lost his life in Afghanistan a month after his third deployment. Five years older than Dani, Micah was her hero and best friend. Even after he married Abby, the three of them continued to do almost everything together. Dani had even been at Abby's apartment when the soldiers appeared at the door to tell them of Micah's death.

Dani wiped away the tears as she thought about Abby. Her sister-in-law was almost seven months pregnant when they received the news about Micah. The weak heart she had as a child deteriorated with her pregnancy, and the doctor had already ordered her to bed. Still, she had been determined she would go to Arlington National Cemetery where Micah always wanted to be buried. *It just wasn't supposed to be this soon.*

George McMichaels, Dani's father, arranged for a private ambulance to transport Abby, making the trip to and from Virginia easier. Dani rode with her friend to keep her company while her parents flew.

On the way home from the airport, Danielle's parents were killed in a hit and run accident. A car had swerved into their lane of traffic, forcing them off of a bridge. Abby's own parents had been killed in an auto accident three years prior, making the trauma much harder for both ladies to bear. The pregnant woman's condition continued to worsen until the doctors put her in the hospital. They told Dani the shock of losing family members so quickly brought on more complications. Abby died giving birth to Micah Clay Lucas Jr. The baby and his aunt were the only family each of them had left.

People offered all types of advice to Dani once they discovered she was appointed guardianship over her nephew. Several friends recommended nannies and others suggested day care centers specializing in caring for infants. Only Amanda Black supported Dani when she decided to adopt Micah and move to Lincks, Missouri. Amanda was her best friend, closer than most sisters. Even though she could not imagine why Dani would want to move to such a small town, Amanda encouraged her friend to follow her heart.

Dani's favorite childhood memories were of the small town and the cottage where her family vacationed at the lake close to Lincks. She did not want to raise Micah in Chicago; it was nothing but painful memories for her now. She was determined to give her new son the happy memories she and her half-brother shared even if it meant raising the baby alone.

She thought about the man her father had promised would find her one day. Someone who would love her with the same unconditional love Micah had for Abby. Dani was not sure that man even existed. *I doubt if Prince Charming lives in a town of six thousand people. Even if he did, would he be ready for an instant family?*

She had not spent much time talking to God lately. She knew she was angry with Him even before Micah's birth. But as the pain became more tolerable, her bitterness toward God faded. She needed God's help to build a new life and to find peace. *I might not find Prince Charming, but I hope I can find God, again.*

As the afternoon turned to early evening, a rest area sign came into view. Dani decided to stop for a minute to check on Micah. He was fussy and probably hungry. She pulled into the parking place nearest to the restrooms. The baby would need a diaper change, and she was ready for a break herself.

With her wallet and cell phone already in the diaper bag, Dani had no need for a purse. She dropped the keys into one of the outside pockets and opened the back door of the vehicle to lift the baby carrier from the seat. Stepping to the trunk of the car, she removed a bottle from the ice chest. Although the distilled water and powdered formula were in a sack in the trunk, she made bottles earlier and put them in ice to make feeding him easier.

"Are you ready to eat, Micah?" Dani asked the infant as she walked toward the building. She never noticed the smiles of the women and men as they passed. Women heard her talking to the baby, bringing a grin to their faces, while most of the men who smiled at her were simply looking at the beautiful woman with the long, brown hair.

After changing Micah's diaper, Dani ran water over the bottle. She managed to bring the milk closer to room temperature, and hoped Micah would be hungry enough to take the less than warm bottle. She carried everything to a picnic table close to her car. Unstrapping the baby, Dani lifted him into her arms and enjoyed the sensation of holding her son. As he stirred, she reached for the bottle. She would have been content to sit there with Micah in her arms for hours, but she needed to get back onto the road.

The summer days meant sunset was still a couple of hours away, but the traveler hoped to reach her destination before then. They were about sixty miles from the exit to Lincks, according to the map. As Micah ate, Dani enjoyed the tranquility surrounding her. She shut out the noises of vehicles entering and exiting the rest area. Soon she started talking to Micah again, as though he could understand every word. She told the baby how good he had been during the trip and how much she appreciated him sleeping four to five hours at a time.

The new mother told Micah about Lincks, the place they would soon call home. Her family had vacationed at the lake near the town every year until she turned thirteen. After that, her family never returned and her parents would never discuss why. She was thankful the cottage she remembered as a child was available although the gentleman she spoke with did not seem to know her family. No matter, she would be there soon to arrange things for herself. He said she could rent the house, and that was all she needed to know at the moment. She shared her favorite memories with Micah, describing the times her family had spent on the lake and visiting the shops in town. *Would it be the same as when I was a child?* As she watched Micah eat, she considered the move she was making. The decision to leave was made in haste, but with prayer. Dani usually made decisions quickly. Thankfully she seldom regretted one once she made them, and hoped it would be the same this time.

She had left a good paying job as director of a preschool in one of the Chicago suburbs to begin a new career in a small town. The pay was much less, but she was assured the cost of living would be lower, also. Teaching second grade was going to be a whole new experience. For the first time, Dani wondered if she had lost her senses, taking the position. Was she ready to teach a classroom of students? As she brushed a strand of hair from her face, she knew there was no other choice. She needed to start fresh for herself and Micah.

Loading the baby into the car, she climbed into the front seat. Her cell phone buzzed with a voicemail. Before she started the engine, she found the phone in the bag and checked to see who had called. It was a solicitor. She deleted the message and tossed the phone in the passenger seat. She backed out of the parking space, ready to be on the highway.

Chapter Two

After being away on business for two days, Adam Reynolds was anxious to return home to his wife, Ami. He had not slept much and found himself nodding off at the wheel. Exiting the highway as the rest area sign came into view, Adam followed a car into the turnoff and parked next to it. He noticed the person in the vehicle was a woman, but little else. He walked into the building and quickly washed his face.

Starting back toward the truck, he moved past the woman carrying a baby in the carrier as she headed for the restrooms. Adam heard her call him Micah, the same name as his son. His heart beat faster as he looked at the infant in the carrier. Ami wanted a baby so badly. It didn't seem fair. They loved God and knew He had a plan for their lives. He just couldn't see anything good in the way their lives were destroyed by events in the last few months. Was this child their second chance? Maybe God wanted to give them this baby. He and Ami could be great parents to Micah. Was this a sign from God?

The woman, carrying the infant, grinned as she walked past him. Adam realized he was still standing in the middle of the sidewalk staring, when another man brushed his arm to step around him. Mechanically he walked to the pickup, but couldn't make himself leave. When she sat the carrier on the table close to his truck, she crooned to the baby in a soothing voice. He had waited so long to hear those sounds. *She said they were going to Lincks? Did I hear her correctly?*

He did not pull from the parking space until she began packing up everything. Adam backed the truck into the lane and drove away from the vehicle. Before the on-ramp appeared, he pulled the pickup over. He needed to follow her to see where they were going.

The red sedan moved out toward the interstate, building up speed as it turned onto the highway. Adam flipped on his signal and maneuvered in behind her car. Traffic was light, so he lowered his speed to stay with her. Forty-five minutes later, he saw her signal to take the Rachele, Lincks exit. Yet another sign! This was his turn-off as well. Letting off the gas a bit more, he waited for her to reach the end of the off-ramp and make the turn. Was she going to Rachele or Lincks? She turned right into the hills. Knowing the road was two lanes from there, he sat at the intersection for a moment to give her more space. He *had* heard her correctly; he also headed toward Lincks.

Rubbing his hand across his face, Adam gave no thought to how people used to tease him about his eyes sparkling, especially when he talked about his Ami. Now if people noticed him at all, it was only tired, sad eyes they looked into, hooded by the grief he felt. His blond hair needed cut, a job Ami used to do for him. A tear rolled down his cheek as he thought about her. *Why God? Why did this have to happen?* Both of them were so excited, when they found out Ami was pregnant. They prayed for their son, thanked God every night for the pregnancy, and went to church every week, but still it happened. What did they do wrong?

He had asked Reverend Jenkins why God let Micah die and let Ami become sick. The Pastor told Adam God hurts just as much as we do when bad things happen, but what we want is not always in His plan. God knows what is best for us. Adam did not believe that. God could have let them live. He did not have to take everything. So maybe God was sorry and wanted Micah to be their son. Adam felt a rush of excitement, God showed him Micah at the rest stop and they were going the same direction. *Give me another sign here, God.*

Unexpectedly, the red sedan careened off of the road and over the embankment. *What happened?* Looking back at the road, he saw a deer stand up on wobbly legs and limp away. Pulling onto the shoulder, he prayed the woman and baby were both okay. Then he thanked God for giving Micah back to them. *I'm sure this is the final sign. I'll take good care of him.*

Checking for traffic, he realized no cars had passed them since exiting the highway. He raced down the rough path carved by the damaged vehicle. Noticing the window was down made it easier to check on them. He popped the locks and opened the driver door and pushed the airbag away from her face. He felt her faint pulse and knew she was alive. Her left arm dangled awkwardly, but he saw no other signs of trauma.

The baby was fussing as he opened the back door. Adam unbuckled the seat belt holding the car seat in place, and lifted the entire system out of the vehicle in one swoop.

"I'll take good care of Micah for you. He'll be safe." He didn't know why he spoke to the unconscious figure. A part of him knew he was doing wrong, but God had given him the signs. His only thoughts were of Ami. He wanted her to be happy again. He popped the trunk lock beside the woman's leg. He figured she had to have food for the infant somewhere. There were three bottles in an ice chest along with a bag of formula and water in front of the container. Putting the bottles in the sack, he picked it up and moved to the other side of the car for the diaper bag.

As he lifted the diaper bag to his shoulder, a cell phone rang; it was laying on the floorboard. Adam dropped the device in with the baby's things. He felt the car slip as he moved from the door. He reached back in, switched off the motor, and put the transmission into park before allowing the door to shut behind him. He had to leave before someone came by. He started up the hill with everything he found belonging to the child.

Strapping the baby into the truck, Adam climbed in. As he glanced down the hill, he realized no one would notice the car in time to help her. He pulled back onto the road, remembering the quiet voice of the woman talking to Micah at the rest stop. As much as he wanted this baby, he could not leave the mother without calling for help. He picked up his phone, only to drop it back into his pocket. They would identify his phone number instantly. Adam reached into the diaper bag and pulled out the cell phone he dropped on top of the other things. He placed his hand across the speaker before he called the sheriff's office. "I think I saw a car in the ravine on the road going into Lincks. Someone might want to check it out." He could not say too much, afraid the dispatcher might recognize his voice. He closed the cell phone and dropped it back into the bag.

Adam talked to Micah during the rest of the drive home. They were not far, but it was all he could do to keep his eyes on the road, and not watch his new son. Adam pulled the pickup into the garage and shut the door. He had to leave the baby in the truck until he could get Jolene out of the house. She had been such a blessing to them; they could not have found a nurse that loved and cared for Ami more.

As he walked in the door to the kitchen, he called out her name. Jolene met him in the hallway. "How is she doing today?" Adam asked the white-haired woman.

"It was a quiet day; she was waiting for you. She'll be happy you're home," Jolene told him.

Adam thanked her for staying. "We won't need you for a few days. I took the next week off work. I want to be with her as much as possible."

"Good. I'm sorry, Adam. If there is anything I can do, please let me know."

"Thanks. I'll call if something happens."

The nurse had been expecting Adam and had everything ready to leave when he came home. She quickly gathered her suitcase and purse. As she left the house, Jolene reminded him to call if he needed her.

After watching the woman back out of the drive and pull onto the road, he raced to bring Micah into the house. Once inside, he would figure out how to get all of those straps unbuckled. He stored the bottles in the refrigerator and turned to Micah. His hands trembled as he pushed the button lying in the middle of the baby's chest. Straps popped loose and Adam grinned. *This isn't going to be so hard after all.* He reached into the carrier as gently as possible, marveling as his big hands swallowed the tiny infant lying there. He brought him to his chest as tears of joy rolled down his face. He turned with his small bundle toward the bedroom.

Ami was lying in the bed, propped up with pillows. As he looked at his wife, he noticed how gaunt her face looked. Adam thought about how her curves used to fit him, as if they were two halves of one whole. Now she was so thin, she had no shape. Her bones protruded against her skin. He looked at her once shining brown eyes as they fluttered open; her pain dulling the spark.

Looking into his face glistening with tears, Ami saw something she had missed for several months. Adam's eyes held the sparkle they had when he was happy. She noticed for the first time the bundle he held in his hands. *What in the world?* Adam reached down to kiss her forehead, as he laid the infant beside her.

"Micah is home, Darlin'."

Ami looked at the baby and then at her husband. "Adam, I don't understand. Where did this baby come from?"

Chapter Three

Sally, the evening shift police dispatcher, listened to the call one more time. Why had the caller not stayed on the line long enough to give more information? He did not even leave a name or a location. The Lincks road, as everyone called it, was twenty five miles long, coming into Lincks from the interstate. She called the sheriff on his cell phone.

"We just received a strange call, Garrett. A man said he thought he saw a car in the ravine on the highway. But he didn't give any details other than to say 'someone might want to check it out.' The voice sounded distorted or muffled somehow. Do you want me to send a deputy?"

"No, I'll head that way. If I find anything, I'll let you know." Garrett had been on duty for twelve hours and was ready to get home, but if a car had gone off of the road, someone could be injured, and he was the closest. He turned onto the main street through town and drove south. The accident, if there was one, would probably be toward the interstate. After traveling approximately ten miles along the highway, Garrett spotted something. The sunlight flashed off of the rearview mirror on the car as he passed by the wreckage. The sheriff never would have seen it, if he had not been looking for a vehicle, and had the sun not been setting. *How did the caller see the car just passing by?* There had to be more to it. Garrett called the dispatcher back.

"I found the car, Sally. It's down the hill about ten miles out of town going south." He gave her the number of the closest mile marker. "Send Mike out here and call Lester for me, please. We are going to need a tow truck to get this one out."

"I'm on it, Garrett. Do you know anything about the occupants?"

"No. I'm just now going down. Tell Mike to bring enough help to get people up on a stretcher. Go ahead and contact Owen. I could use an extra pair of eyes at the scene. Thanks, Sally."

As sheriff of Lincks County for the past ten years, Garrett Austin had investigated a number of accidents on this highway. Someone was constantly taking out the guard rails, and there was never enough money in the budget to keep them in good repair. He grabbed his camera and a flashlight from the patrol car, shining the light down the ravine toward the wreck. He prayed for the occupants as the ray of light followed the ground torn up by the vehicle.

Please let these people be alive and not badly injured, God. There was too much damage for the occupants to have escaped unharmed.

As Garrett stepped from the highway toward the path, his flashlight cast a beam onto the shoulder. There were tire tracks where someone had pulled onto the grass and then out again, mashing the vegetation as they drove. Judging from the size of the impression, the vehicle was a pickup. He could not see any foot tracks. The ground was hard from the lack of rain, so he was not surprised. *Why wouldn't they have waited? Maybe they caused the accident?* He quickly took a picture of the tracks. Garrett would look for answers after he checked on the occupants.

Before he made it completely down the hill, he knew the fire truck was almost there from the wail of the siren. From the other direction, he could make out the sound of the deputy a little further away. They would be here to help extract the people soon. His six-foot four-inch frame dodged tree branches as he moved down the ravine until he reached the vehicle. He took a quick look at the back bumper of the car, snapping pictures as he walked around it. No damage there. They were not pushed off of the road anyway.

Surprised the motor was not still running, he made his way around the luxury sedan to the side. Funny, both driver side doors were open. No one was in the back seat and the driver was still belted in the front. The woman's head lay against the headrest, but the airbag was pushed to the side. Garrett felt for her pulse. The heart beat was faint, but stable. *Thank you, God.* He leaned toward her face to detect if there was any sign of alcohol on her breath. She smelled like peppermint.

The sheriff looked from the front seat into the back seat to make sure the woman had been by herself. *Her left arm doesn't look good.* He could see both of her legs when he checked to make sure she was not pinned by the steering column. She moaned softly as he felt for any other broken bones. Walking back around the car, he reached inside the passenger side to shift the transmission. It was already in park and the ignition key had been turned off. *Did she do that before she passed out?* He checked the glove compartment removing the registration and insurance cards. The name on the two forms did not match. The last name was McMichaels, but first names were not the same. He was not sure which name belonged to the victim, if either did.

"Hey Garrett, what do we need to bring down?" Mike called to him.

"We have one injury, an unconscious woman approximately twenty-five years of age. She has a broken arm. Don't know about any other trauma. I think four of us can get her up the hill just fine. She looks pretty small."

As fire chief of the Volunteer Fire Department, Mike Guthrie directed the three-man crew to load the necessary equipment. One of two paramedics in Lincks County, he was called anytime there was an injury accident around the county seat whether he was on duty or not. He sent the men down the incline while he radioed the hospital.

"Lincks Hospital Emergency Room, this is Mike Guthrie. Come in." He waited for a response.

After a few seconds, a female voice answered "Hi, Sugar." The voice belonged to Dr. Cindy Guthrie, Mike's wife.

"Hey, Beautiful. We have a one-injury auto accident, coming your way as soon as we extract her. Garrett confirmed one broken arm. I don't know about any other injuries at this time. I'll give you more information as soon as we bring her up the hill. I'll be in touch."

"Okay. Mike. Be careful. I'll be waiting."

The fire chief snapped the radio back on his belt and headed down after his men. He quickly dealt with the arm, thankful the lady was unconscious. This was not an ordinary break. Then he felt for any other broken bones, knowing Garrett had just finished, but you could never be too careful. It did not hurt to check twice.

"Okay, guys, let's put the neck brace on her, and lift her out very slowly."

Radioing back to the hospital, Mike updated information about the patient. They loaded the young woman onto a backboard, just as another man walked down the hill. "Good timing, Owen. You can help us carry her back up." Owen Jones was one of the deputies in the Sheriff's office. He had been with the force almost ten years. They strapped her to the board, and the five men lifted her up to their waists. The four of them could have carried her no more than she weighed, but Mike was glad for the extra help so he could protect her arm as much as possible.

"Let Cindy know I'll catch up with her as soon as I finish here, Mike."

"I'll do that, Garrett. See you later."

The sheriff checked the car, again. Funny, he couldn't find a purse. *What woman goes driving without a purse?* He hit the release button inside the car to pop the trunk. Inside he found a small suitcase and an ice chest. The container was empty except for cold water which had probably been ice earlier in the day. He walked around to the front of the car and stepped in front of the small tree. It had stopped the car's descent. He laid his hand on the hood to feel the temperature. The metal was still warm. The accident could not have happened more than a little while ago. As he walked back toward the driver side, the beam of light illuminated something caught on the corner of the bumper. He squatted down to examine it further. It was a patch of deer hair. *That must be what caused her to swerve off of the road.* Deer were thick in these woods, and strangers never paid enough attention to the danger, especially when the sun was beginning to set.

He jotted down the out of state tag number and started moving back up the hill taking the suitcase with him.

"Hey Garrett, Lester is here," Owen called from the top of the ravine.

"Give me a minute more, and you can pull it up," Garrett responded. Lester was the tow truck operator and good at his job. He knew to stay out of Garrett's way until he was through collecting any evidence he might need.

"Measure the skid marks for me, please, Owen."

Checking the area with his flashlight, it bothered him he could not find a handbag. He walked back down the slope and checked under the car to see if it been thrown out. Other things baffled him, as well. *This model sedan should have auto-locking doors. Someone would have had to push the release button to unlock the doors and either they flew open, which seemed unlikely judging from the impact or someone opened them. She didn't open the door with her left arm; nor could she have reached around far enough with her right arm to unlock and then open the door. Who opened the doors, turned off the engine and put the transmission in park? Someone had to have come down here after the car came to rest or left from the car.* He hoped she would be conscious enough to give him some answers by the time he reached the hospital.

As he started back up the hill, Garrett stopped to make a call. "Mom, it looks like I will be a while. I have to go to the hospital to check on an accident victim before I can come home. Is Seth doing okay?"

"He's fine; you just do what's needed. He ate dinner and now he's watching a movie before bed. Do you want to speak to him?"

"Sure. Thanks, Mom." Garrett heard his mother call his seven-year-old to the phone. He could almost feel Seth's frustration about having his movie interrupted, but he wanted to tell him goodnight just the same.

"Hi Dad." Seth actually sounded happy to talk to him.

"Hey, Seth, I just wanted to see how your day went. Did you and Grandma have a good time today?"

"Yeah, we had great fun. Jimmy has a big pool. I did two back flips, well almost two back flips. We swam and swam, and then we had pizza for lunch. Grandma bought me an ice cream cone on the way home." Seth yawned as he finished his sentence.

"Sounds like you might be just a little bit tired, huh?"

"Nah. I want to wait up for you," he said as he yawned one more time.

"Well Champ, it might be a while, before I get home tonight. A lady was hurt in a car accident, and I need to see how she is doing."

"Oh, okay. I'll say a prayer for her, too. Goodnight, Dad. I love you."

"Goodnight, Seth. I love you, too, Son."

Garrett reached the road as he ended the call. "As soon as Owen finishes taking pictures, the car is all yours, Lester. Oh yeah, watch for a purse as you pull the car up, will you please? How many women do you know would go driving out of state without a purse?"

"My wife wouldn't go out of the house without her purse and all of the make-up in there. That bag is more valuable to her than me, I reckon." Lester laughed at his own joke. "I'll keep an eye out for it. Want me to tow the car any place special?"

"No, go ahead and take it to your place. I'll call you after I talk to the driver to see where she was going, and what she wants done with the vehicle."

"Okay, I'll take care of it, Garrett. Have a good evening."

"Thanks, Lester. You do the same."

Turning toward the deputy, Garrett asked, "What did you decide about the skid marks, Owen?"

"They were short but dark. I figure she hit the brakes just before she went down the hill. Speed limit on this stretch of the road is fifty-five. Assuming she was going the speed limit and not faster, she would have hit the grass at forty-five to fifty miles per hour, at least. It will be a miracle if she's not hurt worse than the broken arm."

"That's about what I figured, too. I'm certain she swerved trying to miss a deer. Did you notice the tracks made in the grass; where someone drove off the road and then back on? Her car didn't make those. A pickup pulled over here. I imagine he or she was the one who called in the accident. The driver must have gone down to check on her, too. The doors were open. Maybe that's why the purse is missing. If you'll stay to finish processing the scene and make sure Lester gets the car up okay, I'll go over to the hospital to check on the woman."

"Consider it done, Garrett. I'll see you in a few days. Remember, I'm taking four days off to go fishing." Owen advised.

"I recall. You enjoy yourself and come back safe this time. I need you here in one piece." Garrett was referring to the skiing accident Owen had the last time he took a vacation. The men not only worked together, they were also best friends.

As Garrett drove toward the hospital, he thought about his son. *It's just like him to say he would pray without being asked to do so. He really is a great kid.*

Betty Austin, Garrett's mother, had moved in with them to help watch Seth after Marilyn left. She had walked out on them the day after their son's first birthday almost seven years ago. Garrett had not heard anything from Marilyn until late one night the police chief in Springfield called to say she had died in a shooting. He was not certain he had ever really loved her, but he still hated to think she had been killed.

He thought about how young both of them were when they married. Marilyn changed so much from the girl he dated. She wanted him to leave law enforcement, and he wasn't willing to do that. When she became pregnant with Seth, Garrett hoped she would settle down, but it seemed to make things worse. She always wanted to go out and do something "exciting" as she put it.

Garrett shook his head as if to clear the bad memories. Maybe it was seeing the auto victim that brought back the unpleasant thoughts. *The woman was slender with the same long dark hair Marilyn had. She was prettier than Marilyn though.* The sheriff frowned to himself. *Where did that come from? The poor woman was hurt and you're thinking about how pretty she is. You're a mess, man.*

Chapter Four

"Please tell me, Adam. Where did you get this baby?" Ami's voice was just a whisper. She didn't have the strength for anything more. She gazed at the tiny bundle he laid beside her. He was a beautiful baby almost perfect, but he was not hers. "Why do you have this baby?"

"It's Micah, Ami. The hospital finally let him come home. You probably don't remember too much about the day he was born, but he was very sick. He has been in the hospital the last two months. The doctors called yesterday to say he was healthy now, and could come home to us." Adam hated lying to his wife. He hoped she believed enough of the story to trust what he was saying. She deserved these few days with the baby. Adam refused to think about what would happen then. Maybe the infant would give her enough strength to fight harder. Those thoughts were not really fair to think either. Ami had fought hard to live. She chose giving birth to the baby she carried before starting the chemotherapy needed to destroy the cancer. The risk had been too great. The baby had been delivered stillborn, and by then, Ami's cancer had spread throughout her body. That same day, the doctors told Adam she probably had only two months to live. It had been two months and three days.

"I'm going to get his bottle, so you can feed him. Do you feel up to it, Ami?"

As she stared at the baby Adam said was theirs, she nodded her head. "I am pretty sure I can."

As Adam walked from the room, he heard Ami speak to him again. "Why didn't you talk about him? I don't remember you saying anything about Micah being in the hospital?" The words were so soft he could hardly make them out. Knowing he had no answer for her, he left without a word.

After warming the bottle in a pan of water, Adam tested it on his wrist. Having three younger brothers and sisters had taught him how to take care of babies more or less. Anything else he would learn as needed.

His darling Ami tried so hard to stay awake to finish the feeding. Her eyes closed as Micah sucked the last of the milk. Adam reached down and took the baby from her limp arms, placing him gently over his shoulder just as he had seen the woman do hours before. He wondered about her. *Did the sheriff get to her in time?* Garrett Austin was a good man, as well as sheriff. Adam hoped he didn't leave too many clues behind. He tried to remember the scene as he left it, checking off things in his mind. *I closed the trunk, the passenger door closed behind me; I took all of Micah's things out of the car, and the driver's door. Oh, no! I left both driver side doors open. How could I have been that stupid? They will know the woman could not do that. I don't think I left anything they could track back to me, though. It's too late to change anything now.* All he could do was take care of the baby.

Adam carried Micah into the nursery he and Ami had decorated especially for their baby. They had enjoyed shopping for the furniture, going from shop to shop, looking for the right pieces. He had painted the room a pale green and Ami had sewed the bedding and curtains. Micah would enjoy the room as he got older.

The baby fussed, not content with anything Adam did. He walked with him up and down the hallway and around in the kitchen, but nothing seemed to work. Then he thought about the diapers. The poor infant had not been changed in several hours. No wonder he was unhappy. Adam walked into the kitchen, where the diaper bag still sat.

As he searched for a diaper, his hand touched something else. He pulled it out of the diaper bag and knew it was her wallet. The first thing he saw was her driver's license. Her name was Danielle McMichaels from Chicago, Illinois. The wallet contained credit cards and several bills in various denominations. Thinking back to the car, he did not remember seeing a purse in the seat. This might be her only form of identification. Adam knew he should feel guilty, but instead he felt relief. Without identification and the phone, it would be much harder to prove anything she told them.

Besides, he had done all he could to help her. He did not have to call the sheriff. Her cell phone rang, startling him. It stopped just as he found it in the bottom of the bag, where it had settled. Before it could ring another time, he shut off the device. Adam picked up the bag and took it to the nursery. He needed a diaper to get Micah changed.

The doctor stood at the emergency doors of the hospital, as the fireman pulled the truck into the bay. She waited for the men to open the back doors. Peering inside, she saw Mike, looking at her.

"Hi, Sugar," she said. "How's the patient?"

"Hi, Beautiful. She's stable, but hasn't regained consciousness yet. I'm thinking you might want to x-ray her noggin, as well as her arm."

"Oh, are you telling the doctor how to deal with her patient, Chief Guthrie?"

"I would never do that, Dr. Guthrie." Mike threw his hands in the air in mock surrender.

"Well, it sounds like just what the doctor would order. Let's get her into an examining room, so we can see what other injuries she might have before we do those x-rays. Will you take her to room three please, Sarah? What's her name, Mike?"

"Funniest thing, she had no ID, no purse, not anything on her. The paperwork in the car had different names on it; so we'll have to wait until Garrett checks it out to know her name for sure."

"Okay, for now, she is a Jane Doe. Give me a kiss, so you can go back to the boys." Cindy teased him.

Leaning down, he kissed her passionately on the lips. "That's to keep you thinking about me and how much I love you."

"No way will I ever stop thinking about you, my handsome husband. I love you, too. Now go away and let me do my job. I have to think and I can't with you around." Cindy gave him a big grin and turned toward her patient, once again the efficient doctor everyone expected her to be. "Give the boys a kiss from me when you get home, please," she called over her shoulder.

The victim had just been taken to x-ray when Garrett walked through the doors carrying the small suitcase. "Good evening, Cindy. What can you tell me about the patient? Is she conscious yet?"

The doctor grinned back at her friend as he walked toward her with his constant smile and dark blue eyes sparkling. "Hi, Garrett. Your Jane Doe is in x-ray right now. She hasn't regained consciousness yet. You know it could be hours or even a couple of days before she does, if she hit her head as hard as I think she might have."

"I didn't notice any bruising or swelling on her face."

"Sometimes it's more serious, if you can't see any external signs. We'll see what the x-rays show. I'm sure she'll need surgery for her arm."

The sheriff remembered how it was hanging when he found her and had to agree. "Will you do the operation?" Garrett had known Cindy and Mike Guthrie since his family had moved to Lincks, when he was ten. They had all gone to school together. He had been the best man at their wedding and was godfather to their three boys. He also knew Cindy did not like doing surgeries. She much preferred the emergency traumas.

"No, I've already called Dr. Wright. He'll be here in the morning. I'll leave the mundane stuff to him." she said with a grin. "I assume this is her suitcase?"

"Yeah, I checked, but there was no ID in there, either. I am pretty sure her last name is McMichaels, but I am not certain about the first name. I should know more in a couple of days, assuming she does not wake up to tell us first."

"We can change the name on her chart, when you know for sure; meanwhile I'll make sure the suitcase is put in her room. She's not going anywhere. I plan to keep her sedated until after surgery, anyway. You need to go home and get some rest. You look beat."

The sheriff in him wanted to protest, but the man in him was ready to follow the doctor's orders. "Okay. But please call me if there are any changes in her condition, no matter what time it is. Thanks, Cindy." He kissed her cheek and said goodbye, then walked out to the squad car. As he headed home, he called Sally to let her know where he would be.

Not long after Garrett left, the doctor viewed the x-rays. They settled the woman into a private room right outside of the nurse's station, where they could check on her throughout the night. The x-rays confirmed her fears. The arm was broken in three places, and she had a concussion. There was some brain trauma, but thankfully no bleeding. After her brain settled back into place, any residual headaches would diminish. The arm appeared to be her biggest problem. Cindy was thankful she was not the surgeon. The operation required more skill than she had to pin it back in place correctly.

Chapter Five

When the bed dipped beside him, Garrett opened his eyes to see Seth staring at him. He groaned and closed his eyes.

"I saw you open your eyes, Dad. I know you're awake."

"Did you? How are you this morning, Seth?" Garrett tried once more to make his eyes stay open.

The boy climbed onto the bed and tickled his dad. Garrett rolled his son over to the other side and tickled him back.

Soon Seth was twisting back and forth trying to get loose while he was laughing "Hey, not fair. I wasn't ready for you."

"Sorry, champ. Next time I'll warn you I'm going to tickle you like this," Garrett said, as he began to romp with the boy once more. They did not get time like this often. Normally he was up and dressed for work long before Seth was awake.

The clock read seven o'clock. He had not slept this late in a long time. Even on his days off, which were few and far between, the man was an early riser. He had been awake for quite a while last night, thinking about the accident. Normally he was able to lay them all at God's feet and allow Him to handle the problems. This one was different somehow, and Garrett could not decide why.

"What has Grandma made for breakfast this morning?"

"Don't you remember, Dad? It's Sunday; your day to cook. Grandma is sitting on the deck, reading her Bible until you have breakfast ready. I bet she's talking to God. She does that a lot, you know?"

"Yeah, I know. We should all do more talking to God." Garrett was grateful his parents raised him in church. He had given his life to God as a young man and had always tried to do things he hoped would be pleasing to Him. Except for those years he was married to Marilyn, maybe. The fights they had were not pleasing to anyone, but he had already asked and received forgiveness for those.

He and his mom made a deal when she moved into the house. He would prepare breakfast every Wednesday and Sunday morning. Those two days were easier for him to remember, because those were church days. Today, he planned to go by the hospital after the service.

"I'm hungry, Dad."

"Okay, buddy. What do you want to eat this morning?" Garrett asked, knowing full well the answer would be pancakes. Given a choice, pancakes were always his answer. "Do you want banana or chocolate chip?"

Before he started breakfast, Garrett phoned the hospital to check on the patient. It would be afternoon before he would have the opportunity to stop by and he wanted to know how she was doing. He caught Cindy just before she went off duty and was told there was no change. He would see for himself later in the day.

———❦———

By early afternoon, Garrett walked into Miss McMichaels' room. He still did not know if she was Martha or Danielle. She did not wear a ring on her finger and there was no indication she had ever worn one. He thought she was probably Danielle, but it would be tomorrow or later before he could prove it. Meanwhile he sat down in the chair by her bed. The doctors always told him talking to patients helped bring them around sooner. Garrett wanted her to wake up. As he looked at her creamy white complexion and her dark brown hair, he was reminded of the fairy tales he read to Seth when he was younger. *She looks like a princess waiting to be awakened by the Prince. Ugh, I don't even know where that idea came from. This woman gets me thinking all kinds of crazy thoughts.*

Leaving the hospital, he headed for his office to replay the call they had received the night before. After hearing the recording for himself, he knew the caller had distorted his voice. Sally had already traced the number back to the owners of record, George and Martha McMichaels. The phone number they listed in the phone records was now disconnected. All but one number on the account had been closed. It didn't get him any further in identifying the victim as Martha or Danielle. He still didn't know if the car even belonged to her. He tried the number the phone company had listed as active, but the call went straight to voice mail.

Garrett called Deputy Tom Wallace into his office. "Tom, I want you to go to Lester's and dust that red car from last night's accident for finger prints. I know it's a long shot, but something just doesn't seem right.

The sleeping baby was in the crib next to Adam. "You're such a good baby," he remembered hearing the mother say. Her name was Danielle. But Adam did not want to think of her by her name. It made her feel too real. He knew how easy it was to care for the infant. Micah had slept five hours last night, before fussing for food. Still Adam had a hard time going to sleep. His mind kept seeing her in the car. He knew God was speaking to him, but he did not want to listen. Instead he got up from the chair, where he had slept next to Micah's crib and tiptoed into the bedroom to check on Ami.

Her eyes fluttered and finally opened as she heard him come into the room. She smiled at him. "Adam, I had a beautiful dream last night. I held Micah in my arms. Then God told me He had to take him back. Another mother was looking for her baby. I was sad, but it was so wonderful to hold him, I didn't really mind. I wish you could have seen him and held him, Adam. He was just perfect." Her face was content and the pain seemed far away. It scared him when her eyes closed. Her breathing became so shallow. *No God, not yet. Please, not yet.* Then Adam saw her chest move and he exhaled.

Did she not remember holding Micah last night or did she think it was just a dream? Please, let her enjoy this time with Micah and then I will pay whatever price You ask of me. I just need a few more days, please.

He heard Micah fussing. He was ready for a bottle and a clean diaper. As he changed the diaper, Adam whispered to Micah, "We need to be patient with your Mama. She's trying so hard to stay awake so she can be with you, but it's not always easy. She cares about you so much, though. We both love you, Micah." Then he sat down to feed the baby in his arms and wait for Ami to wake up long enough to smile at them once more.

Chapter Six

It was Wednesday morning before Garrett had most of the answers to his questions. He had never had so many problems accessing information on a person before. The cell phone was a dead end. It had been turned off, or the battery had run down. It seemed like he ran into roadblocks with every person he talked to. The police in Chicago could not locate either a Danielle or Martha McMichaels in the area. The house listed on the registration had been sold two months ago and there was no forwarding address for the sellers.

The car was registered to George and Martha McMichaels from Chicago, Illinois, and they were recently deceased, killed in a hit and run accident about four months ago. A request was in the works to transfer the title to Danielle McMichaels, listed as their daughter. The insurance form in the glove box showed Danielle McMichaels as the insured.

Fingerprints and DNA information had taken a long to receive. There was nothing in the criminal data bases. He had just received notice the prints belonged to Danielle McMichaels. They had been filed by her previous employer, Briarwood Early Learning Center. The other sets of prints found on the vehicle did not show up in any data base Garrett checked.

The requested copy of her driver's license came through on the fax machine. It confirmed her identity as Danielle McMichaels, age twenty-five. She was the woman lying in the

kidnapping, or had she left the baby some place before coming into town? He needed her to wake up and give him some answers.

He reached for the phone to call the hospital. After talking to Cindy, he was more confused than ever. Dani McMichaels had never been pregnant.

Minutes after talking to Ms. Black, the moving company called. They had spent the night at a rest stop and should be in town in little more than an hour. He gave the driver directions to the office and told him a location to park when they arrived. In the meantime, he had less than two hours to find where Dani McMichaels planned to call home.

Garrett had no success calling local realtors to see if they had rented or sold any property to someone by that name. He thought about properties he knew were vacant and might be available. With the lake just outside of town, there were a lot of cabins in the area not inhabited on a regular basis. Garrett decided to walk over and visit with the owner of Lucas' Deli. Maybe he knew of a place for rent or sale.

As he walked through the door of the deli, he looked around for his friend.

"Hi, Garrett, how are you doing? Betty told me about the accident victim you've been checking on. Any leads yet?"

Lucas had moved to town twelve years ago. He and Betty had been seeing each other several times a week for the last three years. Garrett often wondered if their relationship would be more serious, if his mother did not have Seth and him to consider. She insisted they were just friends, but he was not convinced.

"I'm good, Lucas. I'm still looking into the accident. I make a little headway and then run into more questions. I know her name now, but can't get much further. Seems she was moving to Lincks. But I don't know where."

"That reminds me. I hadn't thought to mention this before, but a young woman called me a month or so ago, wanting to lease my parent's place on the lake. The caller said her family used to stay at the cabin when she was younger. Mom rented the property in the summers before she passed away. I haven't used it since building the house in town last year. I liked the idea of someone living there, so I had a cleaning crew go in and spruce up the place just last week. I wrote her name down here somewhere." Lucas started shuffling though a stack of papers. "Here it is. She said her name was Dani something and she was moving here from Chicago. I never did catch her last name, though. Do you think it's the same girl?"

Garrett felt himself relax as he heard Lucas comment. "It must be. All of the pieces fit. The car was registered to George and Martha McMichaels from Chicago. The moving company just called, looking for Danielle McMichaels." Garrett noticed the shop owner turn pale as he grabbed the edge of the counter. "Are you alright, Lucas?"

"Did you say the car was registered to Martha McMichaels? That was the name of my ex-wife after she remarried. I knew she moved to Chicago, but I didn't ever hear anything more." Lucas was shaken by the name.

Garrett took him by the arm and together they walked to the nearest table. The rest of what he knew would affect his friend further. "Lucas, the couple was killed in a hit and run accident about four months ago."

The man sat staring into space for a couple of minutes and then turned to the Sheriff. "Do you remember the talk we had about three years ago? Before I started dating your mother, I wanted you to know about my past and I figured you would investigate me, anyway." Lucas and Garrett both grinned.

"There was more to my past I didn't share with you. It wasn't in my record, so it didn't seem like anybody else's business. Only Betty knows about it; I didn't want secrets between us. Thirty years ago I went to prison for five years for second degree manslaughter, that part you knew. You also knew I used to have an alcohol problem. Anyway, I was in a bar drinking. The guy next to me was talking all kinds of trash, and I told him to 'shut up.' He stood and started to take a punch at me, but I was faster and hit him first. He fell backward; hit his head on a table, killing him instantly. The public defender just wanted the case over and told me my best option was to plead guilty. The judge gave me five years and five years' probation since I didn't have a record. I haven't touched a drop of liquor since.

"The part I never told you before, you probably should hear now. I was married then. In fact, it was one reason I was in the bar that night, to celebrate the birth of my son Micah Clay Lucas. I got to hold him one time in my life, Garrett. I was never allowed to see him again. My wife's parents came and moved them to Chicago the morning after I was arrested. We were never good together, but I loved my son. I wanted to be a good dad for him. It sure didn't turn out like I thought it would. I still think about him all the time.

"My wife's name was Martha. The only reason I knew she remarried was because she wrote me a letter, asking me to sign divorce papers. She said she met someone who made her happy and loved Micah. His name was George McMichaels. I never knew what happened and didn't figure I had the right to know. I had screwed up my life and got what I deserved. No sense ruining their lives as well." Lucas dropped his head.

"I remember the talk we had about the time you spent in prison. I'm so sorry about your son, though. You should have been able to see him after you were released. Maybe it's not too late. He might like to know what a great guy his dad is."

"Thanks, that means a lot, but I don't know. It's been thirty years. Anyway, we kind of got off the subject. What do we do about this Dani? Is she getting better? It makes me wonder what her relationship to Martha was. I don't think those names would be just a coincidence, do you?"

"The woman must be Martha's daughter or her step-daughter." Garrett showed the print of the driver's license to him.

Lucas stared at the picture. "She doesn't look much like Martha. My ex had light red hair with hazel eyes and a face covered in freckles. This gal is certainly pretty. I'm anxious to meet her and hear her story."

"The last time I checked with the hospital, she was still unconscious. Think I'll go over there now to see if there is any change. Would it be okay if I have the movers take her things to the cottage when they get here?"

"I'll get someone to cover the deli and take them to the place myself. Least we can do is get her moved in."

"Thanks, Lucas. I'll talk to you later." Garrett knew Lucas needed time to think. The information he had received affected him deeply. He did not mention the baby. How could he find out if there was a baby with her, or if the child was somewhere else? Was it a coincidence Lucas' son and the baby Amanda Black talked about had the same first name? Dani was the only one with answers.

As the sheriff headed toward the hospital, he called Jane and told her to have the men go to the deli.

He knew Lucas would make them a sandwich, before taking them to the cottage. His friend had paid a high price for his mistake. Garrett was happy his mother had such a good person in her life and she was there for him.

Walking through the hospital doors, Garrett spotted Cindy at the nurse's station. He knew she had been checking on Dani as well. He told her about receiving the driver's license photo confirming Danielle's identity. Cindy stopped at the nurse's station to let them know she was taking a quick break and to page her if they needed anything. They walked to Dani's room together. Danielle looked so peaceful lying in the bed. The doctors could not explain why she had not regained consciousness. X-rays showed the concussion was better.

The doctor and sheriff talked a few minutes outside of the room, until Cindy was paged over the intercom. "Duty calls. Talk to her. Hopefully she'll wake soon. I'll see you later."

Moving a chair close to the bed, Garrett started speaking to the patient. Something seemed to be drawing him to her, and he was anxious to see those eyes open. He talked about his mother, Seth, and the place where she would be living. The cottage was just down the road from his home; so they would be neighbors. The thought brought a smile to his face and he wondered why. *You're just lonesome for a woman, buddy.* But that was not really true. There were quite a few women in town who would go out with him any time he asked. He just was not interested in asking. *Then why is Dani causing these thoughts?* He did not have an answer. He needed to get back to the station. He had already stayed much longer than he had intended.

As Garrett stood by her bed, willing himself to leave, he brushed the random hairs from her face. He rubbed her cheek with his hand, feeling the softness of her skin against his. The thought crossed his mind, again. *She looks like a princess waiting to be kissed.* Before he realized what he was doing, Garrett leaned down and brushed his lips across Dani's. They were so warm he applied just a bit more pressure and felt her lips respond to his kiss. He pulled back to gaze into the most beautiful eyes he had ever seen. They were like pools of liquid chocolate.

"Are you my Prince Charming?" Dani sighed as her eyes fluttered closed.

Garrett did not know what to think. Her eyes opened and she spoke, but now she was asleep. He wanted to pull her into his arms and kiss her until she woke up again. He stepped back from the bed. *What has gotten into me? I can't go around kissing unconscious women. I just hope no one was watching.*

Chapter Seven

Dani opened her eyes and looked around. *Where am I?* As she tried to sit up, she was not sure which hurt worse, her head or her arm. Then she noticed the cast. *What happened?* Her thoughts seemed so foggy, except for the handsome man who had kissed her. She closed her eyes, hoping it was all a bad dream. Well, maybe not all of it was a bad dream. Her eyes flew open a second time when she thought about Micah. *Where is he, is he okay? I have to find him.* She tried to get out of bed, but there were wires and tubes and...the nurse telling her she could not get up.

"How are you feeling? You kept us waiting quite a while before you decided to wake up," the nurse rattled on. Dani's head hurt and she only wanted to find out about Micah.

"Where's my son? Where's Micah?" Dani was distraught, afraid something had happened.

The nurse looked perplexed and told her she would see what information she could obtain. She stepped to the nurse's station and paged "Sheriff Austin to room #104". She had just seen him leave the room. Within seconds, Garrett stepped back through the hospital doors as the nurse walked toward him.

"The patient is awake, but she is insisting she needs to find her son."

As Garrett walked into the room, Dani looked at him with hurt in those big, beautiful eyes. It was all he could do to stop himself from holding her until the pain eased.

"Glad to see you're finally awake. I'm Sheriff Garrett Austin. Can you tell me your name?"

"Dani McMichaels."

"Do you feel like answering a couple of questions, Dani?"

Looking at Garrett, Dani felt herself blush. He looked just like the handsome man in her dream. But nothing else mattered now. She had to know about Micah. "Please, Sheriff, tell me where my son is."

"Do you remember the accident, Dani? You were alone in the car when you drove off of the road. We didn't find any evidence of someone else in the vehicle." He thought about the doors standing open on the car. He watched her expression as the woman closed her eyes, struggling to remain calm.

Then Dani glared at him. Flecks of green flashed in her eyes. "Sir, I was not alone. My baby was in the back seat. Micah is two months old. He couldn't just get up and walk away. I don't know what's going on here, but I assure you my son was with me in the car. We were on our way to Lincks.

"Oh, the deer, a deer ran in front of me, as I came around the curve. I swerved to miss it. I remember the car went off the side of the road. Micah was fastened in his car seat correctly though; he couldn't have been thrown out." Her voice trembled, on the brink of panic. She took deep breaths to keep control. Then she remembered something else. "There was a man. He said not to worry about Micah; he would take good care of him. Please ask him to bring him to me. I need to hold my baby." The tears ran down her face.

When she began to cry, Garrett stood and pulled her body against his chest. He cradled her until she no longer sobbed.

"I'm sorry. I don't usually break down like this. I need information about my son. Do you know where Micah is?"

Garrett would give anything to produce the baby for Dani. It was more than just his job. He wanted to please this woman. *The baby must have been in the car, when she had the accident. That meant someone took him. But why?* He needed more information to go on before he could start an investigation. "Dani, tell me everything you can think of about the man at the accident."

She thought of bits and pieces, but couldn't see the man in her mind. *What's going on? Why would someone take my son? I don't even know anyone in town.* "I don't remember anything else about him. I can't remember anything after hearing his voice."

"Did his voice sound old or younger? Was it deep or higher pitched?"

Dani tried to replay his words in her head. "He wasn't old. His voice was a little shaky but masculine, like yours." She blushed a second time.

"Do you have a picture of Micah?"

"Yes, there are pictures in my wallet. It's in Micah's diaper bag."

Garrett knew she didn't understand what he tried to tell her without saying the words. "Dani, there was nothing in the vehicle to show Micah was with you. There was no diaper bag or anything else." He frowned as he watched how deeply the information affected her. "We need to get a picture of your son."

She fought the panic as she thought, "There are pictures in my boxes. The nurse told me it's Wednesday. The movers should be here already. They were due here on Saturday. Will you look for them? We have to find Micah."

"Will you trust me to do everything I can to find your son, Dani?" He paused as he watched her consider, before nodding her head. "Good. His name is Micah McMichaels, right? You said he is two months old?"

"No, his name is Micah Clay Lucas Jr. and yes, he's two months old."

The same name Lucas said earlier today. This case has more turns than I can keep up with. "So you and the baby's father weren't married?" Garrett ventured to ask.

"Oh, no. Micah's father was my half-brother. He and Abby, his wife, were expecting a baby, when Micah was sent to

Afghanistan. He was killed in action a month after arriving there. My parents were killed coming home from Micah's funeral. Abby died giving birth to Micah Junior." The tears started rolling down her cheeks. "I adopted their baby and took a job in Lincks to start over. My family spent summers here and I wanted to raise Micah's son with some of those good memories."

"So his last name is different than yours?" Garrett wasn't sure he understood.

"When I adopted him, I didn't change his name. I wanted him to know who his father was and to be proud of him." Dani didn't care if it made sense to others. It would to her son one day.

Hearing everything this woman had gone through in the last few months, Garrett wanted more than anything to ease her pain. He had lost so many days since the accident. He needed to find the picture and send out an Amber Alert. He just hoped it wasn't too late.

You know where this baby is and who has him, God. Please help me find him and return him safely to his mother.

The sheriff told her he would be in touch as soon as he knew anything. She thanked him as he left the room. Her eyes glistened with tears. He had to leave to keep from holding her again. What had gotten into him, anyway? He was acting more like a teenager than a thirty-four-year-old man.

As he left the hospital, he pulled out his cell phone and started making calls. The first was Lucas. He wanted to make sure he was still at the cottage. Then he contacted his mom and asked her to meet him there. He explained the situation to her and asked her to let Lucas know about his son. "We need to find his grandson," Garrett commented as much to himself as to his mother. He figured Lucas could use a shoulder when he heard the information.

Dani wiped the tears away as they fell. She was not the frail person lying in the hospital bed. She called for the nurse.

God was taking care of Micah. She knew it in her heart, but waiting was not in her nature. It was time for her to get out of that bed. She needed to be ready when the sheriff came back with her son.

Chapter Eight

Ami stopped eating days ago. Jolene said it was another sign of things to expect. Life somehow settled into a routine the last five days. Micah seemed content, sleeping well between feedings and was cooing more, when he was awake. He had even smiled a time or two.

Two days after the accident, Adam took the baby with him when he drove to Rachele, where he purchased more diapers and formula. He also picked up a bouncer, some clothes, and distilled water to make more milk for the baby. He hated to leave Ami by herself very long, but he could not take a chance on shopping the local stores. People knew him in town and would ask about Micah. He thought about calling the nurse, but was afraid Ami might say something to her about the baby.

Heating a frozen dinner for himself, he warmed a bottle for the baby. Ami was asleep. He suspected she was slipping in and out of a coma. Jolene said to expect that to happen. She had called a couple of times asking to come by to see Ami and give Adam a break. He refused, saying he wanted this time for just the two of them. Jolene seemed to understand.

After feeding Micah, Adam sat down in front of the television to watch the news. He had not seen anything about the accident or the condition of the woman, knowing it probably would not make the St. Louis news. He had prayed for her, but did not know if God would even listen to him after taking the baby the way he had. He felt it was worth it though. Ami had been more content during the few times she was awake. She enjoyed Adam laying Micah beside her. She would whisper to him as he kicked his feet and made noises, like he was talking back to her. The times just did not last long enough. They would have a few minutes together as a family, and then Ami slipped away from him. Each time he worried it would be the last.

Adam had just about finished his dinner, when the newscaster interrupted the sports with an Amber Alert. Micah's picture popped onto the screen as information was given about his age, coloring, and last known whereabouts.

"The baby is believed to have been taken by a man driving a pickup," the announcer said.

Adam panicked. This would be a state-wide alert meaning the store clerks who had fussed over Micah could see his picture. Would they remember him or was he just another baby? He needed time to think. What should he do now?

The baby's picture appeared on the television screen. Dani felt terrified as she stared at his image. Why hadn't the sheriff warned her about the alert? Just then he walked into the room. She watched as Garrett glanced at the television and then at her face.

"I'm so sorry, I wanted to be here to tell you what was happening, but there wasn't time before the alert went out. They begin broadcasting as soon as they receive the information. It will interrupt viewing all night. We don't know where Micah is right now, but it won't take long to find him. Tips will be pouring in any minute. If we don't hear anything tonight, the State Bureau will take over the investigation in the morning. He's out there and we'll find him." Garrett paused as he thought about everything Dani tried to absorb.

"Are you a Christian?" Garrett asked the question with hesitation. Some people might not appreciate being asked point blank, but he did not have time to waste.

Compassion shown in the man's eyes and she knew he was doing everything he could to help her through this. "Yes, I'm a believer."

"Then, would you allow me to pray with you?"

"I would like that, please." Her voice threatened to break, but she was resolved not to cry. She had already cried enough.

She laid her right hand and the tips of the fingers on her left hand into his. As he prayed, he felt her squeeze his hand tighter. She drew upon his strength and the reassurance his prayer offered her.

As he finished praying, his cell phone rang. "This is Garrett."

She watched his face as he listened to Sally for a couple of minutes, and said he would be right there. Dani knew the call involved Micah by the way Garrett looked at her, while he listened. When he hung up, he told her he had to leave. She reached out and took his arm before he stepped away.

"Stop. If you know where Micah is, I want to go with you."

"It could be a prank call. I'll bring the baby back if the call's legitimate."

"Please let me go. I can tell you know more than you're saying. I need to be there." She searched his face, her eyes pleading with him. "The doctor said I could leave in the morning. I'm sure they will let me go now if you ask them. Don't leave me out of this. Please."

"I'll check with the doctor, but don't get your hopes up, yet. This could mean nothing."

When Garrett walked out of the room to the nurse's station, Dani swung her legs over the side of the bed. She had already been up once this afternoon. To hold Micah again, she was ready to do anything. She knew her suitcase was in the closet. As she stepped over there to get it, the sheriff walked back into the room.

"What do you think you're doing out of bed?"

Dani jumped, when she heard his voice. "You startled me. I had to get my suitcase out, so I could get dressed."

"No one said you were going anywhere."

"I'm not going to lie here waiting for some news. I have to do something." Green flecks flashed in her eyes.

"Okay. The nurse talked to the doctor and he said you can leave tonight if you are with me. But you have to take it easy and listen to me. Will you do that?"

"Yes, Sir." Dani flashed her most charming smile at him and heard the chuckle he tried to hide.

"I'll send the nurse in to help you get dressed." He swung her suitcase onto the bed.

Within fifteen minutes, they were in the Sheriff's office, so Garrett could hear the message for himself. He hit the play button on the recording.

"Tell Garrett that Micah is safe. He's with me. I'll be ready when he gets here."

He recognized the voice instantly and dropped into his chair. "Adam, what have you done?" He did not realize he had said the words aloud until Dani spoke to him.

"You know who has Micah?"

"Come on, let's go," He simply stated. This was probably the worst thing Garrett had faced in his career. As they drove out of town, he explained the situation to Dani in painful, clipped sentences.

———✤———

Adam opened the door as the vehicle pulled into the driveway. He held Micah in his arms. Ami had been asleep all day, and he was unable to wake her. It was almost over for both of them. He watched as Garrett led the woman to the house and waited while she entered ahead of him.

The sheriff spoke first. "Dani, this is Adam Reynolds. Adam, Dani McMichaels is the baby's mother. If you want to sit down, Adam will put Micah into your arm. I don't think you need to be standing while trying to hold the baby with your arm in the cast."

Dani sat as he suggested and Adam laid the sleeping child gently into her good arm. She looked up into his eyes, but he was still looking at Micah as if to fill his mind with enough memories to last a lifetime.

"Why, Adam? You knew you would get caught sooner or later," Garrett asked. It was the question on Dani's mind as well.

Adam told the story from the moment he saw Micah to the things he took as signs and the changes it had made in Ami. He left nothing unsaid. "I knew it was wrong, but I had to give Ami this time with him. I wanted to believe God had changed His mind. I know it's over, now. Micah is leaving and Ami is leaving me, too." Tears rolled down Adams cheeks unchecked. When Garrett looked over at Dani, she was crying, also.

"May I meet your Ami?" Dani asked through her tears. She looked at Garrett extending her arm slightly, signaling him to take her son. She walked to Adam and took his arm. They walked into the bedroom. Garrett followed, but waited outside the door with the baby.

Adam's voice quivered as he looked down on the wife he loved more than life itself. "Don't know if I can reach her anymore."

Dani sat in the chair beside the bed and talked to Ami, as if she were awake. She thanked both of them for taking such good care of her son while she was in the hospital. She told them she did not know what would have happened to Micah if Adam had not helped her at the crash site. She related Micah's story and why she had adopted him. Finally Dani thanked Ami for loving Adam so much and giving him the most important part of her life. Turning to Adam, she whispered something to him. He nodded and sat in the chair she had just left. She walked into the hallway and back to the living room with Garrett, where she turned to face him.

"The Amber Alert was a mistake, Sheriff. It was a misunderstanding. I guess the accident made me forget things. Adam didn't take Micah, I asked him to take care for of my baby until I was better. Micah was just fine all along." Dani looked into Garrett's eyes willing him to accept what she was saying.

Garrett looked back wondering if she really understood the things she was asking him to do. "Kidnapping is a crime, Dani."

"It would be if Adam had kidnapped Micah, but since he didn't, I think we should gather his things, and let Adam have this time with Ami. Is there someone we can call for him?"

"I can call Jolene. She stays with Ami, when Adam is working. I don't know how he got her to stay away these last few days. She loves Ami like a daughter."

"Do you know everyone in town and their business?" Dani asked the question in such an innocent fashion, he could not be offended by it.

"Not everyone, but most of them."

Grinning at him, Dani started moving through the room gathering Micah's possessions. She went into the nursery she had passed when going to meet Ami. She found the diaper bag sitting on the table. Pulling her wallet and cell phone out, she added the extra diapers to the bag, and put the wallet and phone on top of everything.

In the kitchen, she found the bottles in the refrigerator, and the can of formula sitting on the counter. As she turned to re-enter the living room, she realized Garrett had been standing there, watching her. He still held Micah in his arms.

"Is everything in your wallet?" His eyes watched her as she moved to the living room.

"I'm sure it is. I didn't bother to check."

"Look, Dani, this is a very noble thing you're asking, but you can't just pretend it never happened. I took an oath to follow the law. I have to take Adam in for the things he's done. It's not something I want, but I don't have a choice."

"Adam's already paid a huge price, Sheriff."

Dani sat down in the chair, and he handed the baby to her. Dani's face showed how much she loved the child. Fear had threatened to overwhelm her until she saw Micah in Adam's arms. Now she was much more relaxed knowing her son was safe.

———✿———

Garrett opened the door as Jolene walked onto the porch with her suitcase in hand. He knew she would stay with the Reynolds until the end. He picked up the baby carrier and other things and took them out to the squad car. After securing everything, he walked back into the house. Dani and Jolene stood together, Micah in the older woman's arms. Dani had explained about the baby and why they were at the house. Jolene looked at the sheriff, as he walked into the room.

"Can you give Adam until Ami's gone to take him in, Garrett?"

"Of course he will. You just call and we'll be here to help in any way we can." Dani answered for him. "Sheriff, if you'll take Micah and get him strapped in the car seat, I'm going to tell Adam and Ami goodbye. I'll be right there."

The sheriff started to speak and then closed his mouth. He grinned at Jolene and did as he was told. He was not quite sure what had happened, but he would let it be for now. He knew Adam was not going anywhere and agreed he and Ami needed whatever time was left.

Knocking softly, Dani stood at the bedroom entrance. Adam turned and stepped to the door. "I just came to let you know, we're leaving. Thank you for taking such good care of Micah. I'm so very sorry about Ami." Dani stood on tiptoes and hugged his neck.

She turned and left the room as tears began to flow. Jolene patted her shoulder as she walked through the living room. By the time she was outside, she was sobbing as hard as when she thought Micah was gone. She ran into Garrett's waiting arms. He held her close kissing her hair softly. Soon the sobs turned to hiccups, and she brushed her hand across her face. "I seem to be making a habit of getting your shirt all wet, Sheriff," Dani stated through the hiccups.

"I think it's about time you called me Garrett, if we're going to be co-conspirators in this mess, don't you?"

"Thank you, Garrett." Dani responded, her smile deepening to show her dimples. He wanted to taste those beautiful lips again, but he was afraid he would scare her away. Her life seemed so fragile, now.

Chapter Nine

Garrett pulled into the driveway and stopped the car. Surrounded by tall, whispering pines with hints of the lake showing on either side of the house, it was the perfect setting, rustic but elegant. He heard the gasp as Dani caught her breath.

"This is not the cottage I rented. I don't remember everything about it, but it's much smaller than this and not nearly as magnificent."

Knowing Dani would not be happy with the arrangements he had made, he had not told her. Instead, he turned off the ignition, climbed out of the car and walked to the passenger door without replying to her remark. He helped her out of the car.

"Who does this house belong to, Garrett?"

"It's mine. You and Micah are going to be staying here for a few weeks."

"I can't do that. It wouldn't be appropriate and besides, I have a perfectly good home around here, somewhere."

"And just how do you propose to take Micah to this place of yours? Your car is in shambles, remember? You can't carry the baby with your broken arm, and you just got out of the hospital. You're not able to take care of yourself, let alone him. You'll stay here with my mother and son and be a good houseguest." Garrett opened the back door and removed Micah and his carrier.

Dani watched as he grabbed the other things. "I know what you just said is true, but you could have discussed it with me."

He turned toward the house and then looked back over his shoulder. "Did you know your eyes get green flecks in them when you're angry?"

"My dad always told me the green flecks showed when the dragon came alive."

Garrett laughed. "I can tell. I'll have to remember to keep it under control as much as possible. Let's go in so you can meet my mother before she comes looking for us."

Garrett smiled at his mom as she walked out of the kitchen drying her hands on her apron. She was about the same height as Dani with salt and pepper hair styled in a very flattering cut. Her face wore a big smile as she viewed the man and woman walking in the door.

"Mom, this is Dani McMichaels. Dani, meet Betty Austin, the general of this household."

"Welcome to our home, Dani. We're so happy to have you and Micah stay with us for a while. Garrett, if you'll take her things to the bedroom, I'll fix Dani a glass of tea and show her the house. Come with me, dear."

Hesitating, Dani looked at Micah in his carrier.

"I'll bring the baby to you in just a minute. Go with Mom now."

Dani nodded and followed the older woman. "Your home is beautiful, Mrs. Austin. It feels so inviting."

"Please, call me Betty. You and I are going to be spending the next few weeks together, and I know we are going to be good friends." She poured three glasses of tea as she spoke.

"Seth went to church camp this week, but will be home some time tomorrow. We'll enjoy the peace and quiet until then." Betty grinned.

Micah fussed as Garrett carried him into the kitchen. "I think this little guy is hungry. Mom, there are bottles in the diaper bag. If you'll warm one for me, I'll feed him before I head back to the station."

"You're going back to work?" both ladies asked.

"There'll be emails to answer; questions about decisions made today. I can't put off those things. I want to take care of this before it gets too out of hand."

"Then go on, Garrett. Dani can go into the living room with Micah and I'll bring the bottle as soon as it's warm. The sooner you go, the faster you can come home."

Nodding his thanks, he kissed his mother's cheek and carried the baby to the front room, leaving Dani to follow.

"You won't be in trouble about all of this, will you, Garrett?"

Grinning, Garrett looked down at her. "I'm a big boy, Dani. I can handle the situation, whatever happens. Right now, you get some rest. You look exhausted. You just got out of the hospital, and I don't want to take you back." The sheriff laid the infant in Dani's good arm after she sat down. Then he walked to the door. Before closing it, he looked back. "I'll see you in the morning. Get some rest."

⁂

After Micah finished his bottle, the ladies talked about his sleeping arrangements.

"Garrett will bring the crib from the cottage in the morning. For tonight, let's use a dresser drawer for him to sleep in. Babies love small spaces, while they are young anyway. It'll work for him tonight."

Betty saw Dani try to stifle a yawn. "You must be exhausted after all you've been through. Let me finish this, and we'll get you ready for bed. I expect you'll need a little help changing clothes. The cast makes doing everything awkward. I know; I broke my arm a few years ago. It's very frustrating trying to do anything. I'm afraid I snapped at the boys more than once." Betty grinned with an unashamed look on her face. She made quick work of the last blanket, before picking Micah up from the bed. After Dani kissed his cheek and rubbed his head briefly, Betty cuddled him a moment and laid him into the makeshift crib. Clean and fed, she knew he would sleep for a few hours.

It had taken some coaxing, but Dani conceded leaving Micah in Betty's room. "I know I can't care for him properly right now. I can't thank you enough for taking us in like this. Hopefully, it will only be for a few days." She paused as she and Betty walked back into the living room.

"Garrett didn't show me where he put my things." Dani hated to ask, but she had no idea where she was to sleep. Betty's room was a suite just off of the kitchen.

The older lady led Dani toward the bedrooms. "Garrett put you in his room. The third room has a sleeper sofa, and he didn't think you would be comfortable there." Betty looked at Dani, when she stopped suddenly with her mouth open.

"I can't sleep in his room." A look of horror formed on Dani's face, and Betty knew what she was thinking. Garrett had not told her anything about the arrangements they made earlier.

Betty touched Dani's arm, "Garrett is sleeping at your cottage down the road, dear. I took a suitcase of clothing down before you got here. The bed has fresh sheets and the bathroom fresh towels. He will need nothing. He'll come to the house for meals. It makes a perfect arrangement. You're here, where I can help you, and he can come and go without disturbing us, if need be." Betty hoped Dani felt better after knowing a few more details. She turned to enter the bedroom. "You also have clean sheets and towels."

"My goodness, you accomplished so much in a short amount of time. I didn't even realize Garrett had told you about the situation," She paused briefly. "I hope he can smooth things over for Adam." Dani remembered the pain in Adam's face as he looked upon his wife. Ami was so young and was once a beautiful woman from the pictures she had seen in the house. Cancer had stolen everything from her. Death was certainly no stranger to Dani lately, but her heart still ached for the couple.

"Garrett and Adam grew up together. Adam was always at the house hanging out. He and Ami married about the same time Garrett and Marilyn did, but theirs was a much happier union than Garrett's. They tried so long to have children. When she was finally pregnant, I think Adam told the whole county. It was about four months into the pregnancy when Ami began to have problems, and they diagnosed the cancer. She refused to do anything that might jeopardize the baby, so they were waiting to start the treatments. By the time their Micah was delivered, the cancer had spread to the point nothing could be done." Tears filled Betty's eyes and she dabbed them away. She loved Adam like a son.

"They named their baby Micah, also?" Dani asked with a catch in her voice. Adam had not mentioned that.

Betty nodded. "I realized the babies were delivered just two days apart when I saw the Amber Alert," She shared, while collecting the night things from Dani's suitcase. "Now we need to stop these sad thoughts and rejoice because God has brought you and your Micah safely back together."

Betty saw the tears streaming from Dani's eyes. "Oh honey, there's no need to cry. Everything is fine now. Ami will soon be with the Lord and as broken as Adam is right now, he loves God and He will get Adam through this pain, just as He has done for you." Betty comforted Dani with a hug.

"I don't know why I keep crying. Poor Garrett, I soaked his chest twice today." Dani tried to wipe the tears away, but they continued to fall.

Betty giggled, "With Garrett already six foot, four inches tall, I hope all that water won't make him grow anymore." Dani laughed too and hugged Betty a little closer. "Thank you. I love you, already." As the words tumbled out so naturally, Dani bit her lip. She should not be saying those things to a virtual stranger, but she did not feel like a stranger. She really did already love Betty.

Chapter Ten

The call came early the next morning.

"Garrett, this is Jolene. Ami passed away. It was a peaceful death and Adam stayed with her until he had to say goodbye. Now, he's ready to face his consequences," she stumbled through the words.

The sheriff arrived at the house an hour or so after they took Ami to the funeral home. Adam let his friend inside. "I'm so sorry," Garrett whispered as the two men embraced.

He spread his arms wide, as Jolene walked into his hug, coming from the bedroom she had just cleaned. "I sure could use some coffee," he said to her. She nodded, knowing the two men needed time to talk.

Garrett sat beside Adam on the sofa as he heard his friend ask, "When do you want to take me in? Do you think I'll be able to make bail, so I can take care of Ami's funeral?" the words choking Adam as he looked at the floor.

"I've talked to the D.A. and the judge. Because there was an Amber Alert sent out, there'll have to be charges filed. If you're willing to work with the courts, I think we can arrange something. Dani is still insisting she doesn't want kidnapping charges filed. I don't think they'll have any choice though." Garrett had spent time with both officials to see if the charges could be reduced to something less, but they had to follow the law.

"That's more than I deserve. Thank you for everything you've done and will you please thank Dani for me, also? It's hard to believe she'd feel this way after what I did to her."

"After you've been to the funeral home, stop by the station, and we'll get the formal arrest paperwork out of the way. Bail is already covered. We just have to do the booking." Garrett knew, as sheriff, he should take Adam in to process him, but he just could not do it. Adam was not going to leave town and would honor his obligations. After a few more minutes, he was ready to head back home. Adam needed time to grieve by himself.

"Are you going to be alright?" Garrett asked looking at him. The only response was a nod. The men hugged a second time before saying goodbye. He would see Adam later in the day.

Garrett drove to his house. Seth was due home from church camp, and there was more Garrett needed to discuss with Dani before she heard it from someone else. "Anybody home?" he called going through the front door.

Seth ran into his arms. "Hi, Dad."

"Hey, you're home early. Did you have a good time?" Garrett lifted the boy for a hug.

"Yeah, I had a great time. Did you see the baby living in our house? Come look at him. Grandma told me his mom said I could hold him, when I'm sitting down. Grandma said I have to take a shower first, though. I'm ready to hold him right now. He's so little. Was I ever that little?" Seth was talking a mile a minute about Micah.

So much for me worrying he might not appreciate another child in the house. "Where is Grandma and Dani?" Garrett asked.

Seth paused for a breath of air. "Grandma is giving Micah a bath. Who's Dani?"

Frowning, Garrett allowed Seth to take him into the kitchen where Betty was bathing Micah in the sink. She was talking and laughing with him like she did when Seth was little. "Looks like both of you are having fun," he remarked as he watched Micah smile back at the noises made to him.

Betty laughed, "I never realized how much I missed having a baby around the house." Seth and Garrett watched as she lifted Micah from the water onto a towel spread on the counter. She began to dry him as Garrett told her about Ami and Adam.

"Even though he's hurting now, I know God will see him through the pain," Garrett said as he watched his mother dry the baby. "Where's Dani?"

"Oh, we walked up to the cottage this morning to see if we could find some of their things. Dani went back to bring more of their clothing, if she could find the boxes. Seth, do you want to help me get Micah dressed?" He jumped at the chance.

"I'm going over to make sure she doesn't break the other arm. She just can't wait for help, can she?" Garrett headed out the back door and up the lawn toward the cottage. He had not seen her today and already missed her like crazy. He slowed to let his thoughts sink in. *I think I'm falling in love with Dani McMichaels. My heart was lost those hours I sat waiting for her to wake in the hospital. I didn't even know what she was like. I didn't know how kind she was or how stubborn she could be. It doesn't matter, I love everything about her. Can a grown man fall in love so easily and that quickly? I have to slow down before I scare her for sure.* He put his thoughts aside as he reached the cottage door.

Feeling a bit awkward since he was living at the cottage, he decided it would be best if he knocked. Garrett let himself in when he heard Dani call out. As he walked through the living area, he saw her standing on the balcony looking over the lake. The water behind her was tranquil, but there was enough wind to cause the pines to sway, and the dried leaves to rustle. The breeze blew her hair as she stood there, and she pulled it away from her face. Walking into the house, Dani's eyes were red, and the smile she tried to produce failed miserably.

"You've been crying. What's wrong? "

"I've been thinking a lot about my brother today. He would have loved coming back here. We had such good times. I have a lot of wonderful memories with my family. I feel at peace here. But I've also been thinking about Adam. I don't think I can stay in Lincks after all."

"What are you talking about, Dani? I thought you moved here to begin a new life."

"I did, but I can't stay here with Micah, knowing how Adam feels about him."

"Are you worried Adam would try to take him, again? Because I can tell you—"

"No, of course not. I know Adam would never think about something like that. It would just be so unfair for him to have to live so close to Micah, loving him so much."

"So you would be willing to give up your dreams to spare the man more pain, is that what you are telling me?" Garrett's voice grew tight with emotion. He was not ready to let Dani go without at least giving their relationship a chance. But maybe Dani did not feel the same things he felt when he looked at her; the electricity he felt when he touched her.

"Garrett, I don't know what to do. I can't hurt Adam any more, but I don't know if I can go back to Chicago either. I'm so confused."

"You can't go back right away anyway. You'll have to testify at the trial. You don't have a car to drive, even if you were in any shape to travel. Adam would feel horrible if he thought you were running. You also have a teaching position waiting for you here. You wouldn't have a job in Chicago. Please give yourself some time to make a decision."

She hesitated, considering Garrett's statement. "You're right. I'm not in any condition to make decisions today. My emotions are all over the place. Right now, I need to get back to the house and see about Micah. I've been down here far too long looking for boxes of clothing for both of us."

"Did you find the boxes you want to take up to the house?"

Nodding, Dani turned and pointed to the boxes she wanted moved. When she turned back, she collided directly into him with her cast. She heard him gasp as he grabbed her shoulders to keep her from falling. Garrett looked from her eyes, to her lips, and back into her eyes. They turned a shade darker as he began to lower his head toward hers.

Before he reached her mouth, the door flew open and a young boy burst through. They separated instantly. Dani blushed, while Garrett kept his eyes on her face and his hands on her arms as he spoke to the boy. "Seth, it's not polite to come into a person's house without knocking."

"Sorry, Dad. Grandma said you were staying here, and I came over to see why." Then Seth looked at the woman. "Are you the Dani everyone keeps talking about?"

She smiled, "I am and you must be Seth. How do you do?" She stepped out of Garrett's arms and extended her hand to the boy. Seth reached out and shook it just like his dad taught him.

Then Dani answered his first question. "Your dad is staying here, because he very nicely gave up his room, so I could be closer to Micah and would be more comfortable. I can't do much for myself right now with my arm in this cast. Do you mind?"

"Nah, I don't mind. Maybe I could stay here, too. It would be like the girl's dorm and the boy's dorm at camp; Micah's too small to count. He sure is a cute little thing. Can I help take care of him, too? Dad, can I stay down here with you? Oh yeah, I almost forgot, Grandma said to tell you it was time for lunch. She made soup and sandwiches—"

"Whoa! Son, take a breath. Here, take this small box up to the house for me, will you? Tell Grandma we'll be right there."

"What was in that box, Garrett?" Dani asked as Seth scampered back to the house.

"I have no idea. I'll bring it back later, when I get the boxes you wanted. We need to talk about something, but I guess we'd better get back to the house."

As they walked, Garrett told her about Ami, the visit to Adam, and talking to the D.A. and judge. "Adam might have to serve some jail time, but I'll do everything I can to keep it from happening. Thank you for the way you've handled the situation. The D.A. and judge were both surprised at your actions."

"Adam will suffer from this for a long time, Garrett. Jail wouldn't accomplish anything." Dani looked at the man walking beside her.

Nothing more was said as they reached the back door and walked into the kitchen. The man sitting at the breakfast bar caused Dani to gasp, her eyes expressing shock as Garrett glanced at her.

"Micah," she whispered as she fainted. Garrett caught her before she fell to the floor. Swinging her into his arms, he carried her to the sofa.

"Are you alright, Dani?" he asked, as her eyes fluttered open a minute or two later.

The color was coming back into her face, but she still looked distressed. "The man in the kitchen," she whispered, "he looks just like my brother."

"His name is Grant Lucas, but everybody calls him Lucas. He's your Micah's Grandfather; your half-brother was his son. I wanted to talk to you about him at the cottage. I'm sorry I didn't get a chance to explain all of this before you met him."

Dani looked at Garrett. "He can't take Micah from me." The remark was as much a question as a statement.

"No, Dani, he's not here to take Micah, although he would probably love to meet him. Lucas owns a deli in town. He was the one who rented the cottage to you and helped me fit all the pieces together when you were in the hospital. Lucas is one of the good guys."

"He owns the cottage? I thought it was a distant relative of Micah's grandmother. He must have been the reason our parents stopped coming here each year. Mother talked about Grant being Micah's dad, but she always made us think he was dead. Micah never knew his father was alive. How could she have kept that from him?" Dani reached out and wrapped her arm around Garrett's neck seeking his comfort.

Although he would like nothing more than to continue holding her, after a minute he asked if she was ready to meet the man in the other room. They walked back into the kitchen together. "This is Lucas, Dani."

Before he could stand, Dani threw her arm around his neck and hugged him close to her. "I'm so sorry," she whispered over and over. "Micah wanted so much to know his real father. Dad loved him, but could never replace the father Micah needed to know." Dani sobbed while clinging to Lucas. He shed tears in return, as he clung just as hard to her.

"I think you had better let him meet his grandson, Dani," Garrett spoke from behind them. She let go of Lucas, but he kept one hand around her waist, holding her close. Garrett laid Micah in Lucas' free arm. The baby looked at the man's face and grinned.

Chapter Eleven

Sunday morning, Dani woke to Garrett whistling in the kitchen. She quickly took a sponge bath, washing around the cast as best she could, and struggled into clothes for church. She was anxious to attend a service, again. With everything that had happened the last few months, she had gone to church sporadically and missed the fellowship with God. She knew she had stayed away because of the anger she felt after the deaths of her family. She had finally realized she had blamed God for something that grieved Him as much as it did her. She also looked forward to sharing the time with Garrett and his family.

Dani walked into the kitchen to see the sheriff at the stove flipping pancakes. "Good morning." they said in unison.

"Can I get you some coffee?" Garrett turned to get a cup from the cabinet.

"I can get it. Do you want some more?" she asked, and he held out his cup as she finished filling hers.

"Thank you. Mom and Seth are feeding Micah on the deck."

"You're welcome. Is there anything I can do to help with breakfast before I check on Micah?"

"Nope, I have it under control. Go play with your son for a few minutes while I finish."

Dani opened the door and walked onto the deck. Seth was holding Micah with a look of adoration on his face. They looked so cute together. She wished she could capture the moment in a picture. She had not taken very many pictures of Micah and realized she needed to change that. She used to enjoy taking photos in her spare time. Problem was spare time seemed to be at a premium these days.

—————

Two hours later, the group entered the church. Garrett watched Dani's face as she looked around the sanctuary at the stained glass windows and natural wood. She looked more at peace than she had since they located Micah. People came up to them, welcoming her, and saying hello to the family.

Garrett held Micah in the carrier. He took Dani's arm as he headed out of the sanctuary. "Let's get Micah settled in the nursery. Seth has already taken off for Sunday School." He introduced Dani to the ladies in the baby room, laying Micah on a blanket before asking if she was ready to go to class.

She looked up; dimples showing as she smiled. "I'm ready, when you are."

Garrett wanted to take Dani into his arms and hold her forever. He had never been so affected by a woman before. Instead he took her hand as they walked to the Sunday school classroom, and he began to introduce her to the other people in the class.

—————

As they entered the sanctuary for church services, Dani felt God's presence surround her. She and Garrett sat in the third row and Betty and Lucas joined them. The congregation was asked to be seated as the pastor came to the pulpit. Before beginning the sermon, Reverend Jenkins read the prayer requests for the week.

"Martha Schmidt is recovering nicely from her hip surgery. Ralph Andrews wants to thank everyone for helping out when they had the fire at his place last week. We need to remember Adam Reynolds in prayer. Ami's funeral will be held here at the church tomorrow at ten. Let's open our Bibles to Proverbs thirty-one, verses ten through thirty-one. These verses remind me so much of Ami. I know her spirit is with us today." The pastor began to read aloud.

———❀———

"Ladies, I think we should take the boat across the lake and have a picnic," Garrett announced as they walked into the house after church.

"Great idea, Garrett." Betty started pulling items from the refrigerator before Dani had a chance to say anything.

"I don't know if Micah and I should go. He is awfully small and with this cast on my arm..." Dani was not sure she felt like being included with family plans. The more involved she was with all of them, the harder it would be to leave.

"Micah will be just fine and you will, too. I won't let anything happen to either of you." Garrett was not going to take no for an answer. He was determined to spend time with her, even if the family was along.

She did not hesitate long before speaking. "Okay, if you are sure we won't be intruding." Dani let Garrett make plans for her again. "What can I do to help?"

Dani helped Betty prepare a picnic lunch, while Lucas drove home to change clothes. Seth and Garrett were at the dock, getting the boat organized. The ladies quickly changed outfits and Lucas was back by the time they were all ready to go.

"Lucas, would you please carry the picnic basket? Betty said she is going to carry Micah. I can manage the rest," Dani picked up the diaper bag and other bag of things they needed to bring with them.

As they neared the boat, Garrett looked up at the group. His eyes came to rest on Dani with a smile transforming his face. He noticed the red tank top and white shorts. A ponytail swung from behind the white baseball cap like a flag blowing back and forth. Red flip-flops completed the outfit, making her look more like a teenager ready for a day at the beach. Only the cast looked out of place. He walked to the front of the boat to help her aboard, as Lucas helped Betty.

"You look beautiful," Garrett whispered as she brushed past him.

Already blushing from his gaze, his comment made the flush worse. Garrett wore navy blue swim trunks with a white t-shirt. The shirt fit over his broad shoulders making the muscles in his arms and chest quite apparent. She caught herself watching him and only turned away when Seth asked if they were going anytime soon.

Garrett smiled and walked to the driver's seat. "Sit in the seat next to me. We'll put Micah between us."

Lucas untied the ropes and pushed the boat off. Seth and his grandmother sat in the back seats next to Lucas. Garrett started the motor, swung the boat around and headed out across the water. With little, to no rain the last year or so, the lake levels were low, causing Garrett to keep the speed down to avoid hitting anything just under the surface. Soon they reached their destination, a sandy beach on the other side of the lake.

As Garrett pulled up on the shore, Lucas jumped out and tied the rope to a nearby tree. Seth jumped off of the back of the boat and grabbed the two bags Dani had carried with her. Lucas helped Betty onto the shore and took the food basket Garrett handed him before he waded back to retrieve Micah. After unloading everything they needed, Garrett jumped out and reached up to lift Dani into the shallow water beside him. His breath caught as he watched a grin light up her face. He kept his hands spanned around her narrow waist a moment longer than necessary, only releasing her when Seth hollered something.

"This is a beautiful spot for a picnic," she remarked, looking across the beach to the lake.

"We like coming here once or twice a month. Sometimes we come only for an afternoon and sometimes to camp for the weekend. It's not too far from the house, but it makes you feel like you're on an adventure according to Seth." He smiled as they walked to the spot where Betty spread the blanket under a large tree. It provided enough shade to protect the baby.

Dani removed the food from the basket as Garrett took Micah out of his carrier. He would enjoy some 'tummy time' while they ate their lunch. The ladies had prepared sandwiches to go along with the potato salad and baked beans Betty had made the day before. Soon everyone was stuffed.

Garrett stood and offered a hand to Dani. "Come take a walk with me. Seth's already combing the beach for treasures." Dani reached out and took his hand as he pulled her to her feet. He laid his hand on the middle of her back as they walked.

"Tell me about your work, Garrett," Dani encouraged.

The sheriff told her several stories, making her laugh until tears ran down her face. As they came to a large outcropping of rocks, Dani stopped and leaned against them. "I know your job cannot be fun all of the time, but you sure do have some great tales." As she wiped her eyes, she looked up at him to see him looking back at her. She blushed slightly as Garrett leaned toward her, placing a hand on either side of the rocks. She wanted the kiss as much as he did.

"Hey, Dad, where are you?" Seth interrupted.

"My son has the worst timing," Garrett declared as he called out to his son. He grinned at her and offered his hand as he pulled her away from the formation.

"Let's go swimming, please, Dad," Seth asked as they walked back to the beach area. Garrett pulled his t-shirt over his head. Dani watched him as he ran to catch his son in the water. His muscles rippled as they dunked each other; swimming across the water like fish, and having a good time. As Micah stirred, she thought about him growing up without a father to do things with, knowing she would have to be both mother and father to him. *Would it be any easier to raise him in Chicago? Micah had been so much happier here. It's why we came in the first place. The longer I'm around Garrett, the stronger my feelings for him are. Then there is Adam to consider. His feelings are so raw, right now. I can't stand to hurt him any further.*

She did not hear the guys approach until Garrett dripped water on her legs. "Come wading with us. I'll make sure you don't fall in a hole or get in too deep to get your cast wet."

Lucas picked up the baby from the blanket. "Betty and I are taking Micah for a walk. You don't want to sit here all by yourself."

Dani held her hand out to Garrett and allowed him to pull her to her feet. Seth found a Frisbee in one of the storage lockers on the boat and threw it to his dad.

"How good are you at throwing a Frisbee?" Garrett asked, grinning at her.

"Just get out into the water and be prepared to catch it, mister. Micah and I played this all the time."

"Okay, then; dazzle me, lady." Grinning, Garrett told Seth to move to one corner and he moved to the other corner of an imaginary triangle. "Show us what you can do, woman," he taunted her. Dani threw the disc right into his waiting hands. "Not bad; how are you at catching it?"

"If you can throw it straight, I can catch it," she teased him back. The three of them played together until Lucas and Betty walked back into view. As she heard them approach, Dani turned to look in their direction. The Frisbee hit her, knocking her off balance. She sat down in the water, saving her cast from a soaking at the last second. The look of surprise had everyone silenced as Garrett hurried to help her up.

"Did I hurt you?" he asked, trying to not laugh.

"Only my pride." She burst out laughing as the others chuckled along with her.

"I think Micah is ready to head home," Betty told the group. She handed towels to Dani and the others. Together the women packed up the few remaining things as the men loaded everything back into the boat.

Heading back to the house, Dani thought about how much fun she had. *It felt good to be part of a family, again. But this isn't my family, only kind people willing to share their lives for a time. I have to make a future for my son and me. The biggest question is should it be here or in Chicago? God, I need Your guidance more than ever.*

Chapter Twelve

Dani replayed Garrett's question in her mind. He asked her yesterday evening if she was sure she wanted to go to Ami's service. Did she want to go? *No.* After four funerals in six months, another memorial was the last place she wanted to be. But she had to be there for Adam. He had to know people still cared about him and did not think any less of him after what he had done. She could not take Micah, so Lucas volunteered to stay home with the boys.

Adam sat quietly with Jolene sitting beside him. Garrett, Owen, Mike, and three other friends sat across the aisle of the church, serving as pallbearers. Betty and Dani sat in the row behind them. The church filled to capacity, all there to bid Ami a final farewell.

Reverend Jenkins faced the mourners with a smile on his face. "Ami Reynolds loved the Lord as much as any person I know. She didn't just talk about her love for God, she lived it every day. We talked often about His plans for her life, and somehow, I think Ami knew hers would not be a long life on Earth. She looked forward to eternal life in heaven. I know she is rejoicing right now with her son and with Jesus. She would not want us to grieve for her passing, but to make sure our life was in order to one day be with her again. Let us pray."

Several people stepped forward one by one to eulogize their friend. After the service ended, Dani walked up to Adam. He reached out, and hugged her for several seconds, as they cried silently together. No words were ever exchanged, but the pain of losing loved ones seemed to forge a bond between the two. Dani thought about how painful it would be for Adam to know they were in the same town.

———⚜———

The next day, Dani had an appointment with the doctor who had performed her surgery. While Betty drove to the doctor, Dani admired the scenery. This area was beautiful with the tall pines and various trees mixing with the rock formations. Some trees had already begun to lose their leaves. Fall would not be as spectacular as normal due to the lack of rain. The temperatures had been higher this summer than usual as well, adding to the drought conditions. As the car drove past the area similar to where Dani's car had gone off of the road, her thoughts turned to Adam.

He had appeared in court earlier that morning. After accepting his guilty plea, the judge called Dani to the witness stand.

"Ms. McMichaels, do you still want the court to believe you do not want to see Mr. Reynolds punished for the crime for which he has just confessed? Do you truly forgive this man?"

"Your Honor, I do forgive Adam Reynolds. Jesus forgave my sins and wants me to do the same. Adam is only guilty of loving his wife so much; that he was willing to accept any punishment handed down to bring a few days of happiness to Ami. Surely, this is a crime that can be exonerated."

The judge looked into Dani's eyes as she made the statement. Then he looked across the chamber at the people present, shaking his head slightly.

"Thank you, Ms. McMichaels. Mr. Reynolds, you will please rise. In light of the statement just made by this extraordinary woman, I'm going to sentence you to five years' probation. I also require you to enter into counseling for a period of no less than six months."

Adam showed little emotion after the verdict, but thanked Dani for her part in the proceedings.

As she thought about the trial, she said a quick prayer, asking God to bring him a measure of comfort in the months ahead. She did not understand why God brought Adam into her life, but she knew there was a reason.

Betty's voice broke into her thoughts, "Are you looking forward to classes beginning, Dani?" she asked without taking her eyes off the road ahead. None of them had talked very much about the upcoming school year and her new position. With everything else happening, the job seemed almost surreal.

"I think I am, Betty. Being in charge of the preschool, I wasn't able to interact with children as much as I would have liked. I hope it will be easier working with children, than it was with the parents a lot of the time," she stated smiling. "I would hate to leave the school system without a teacher at the last minute, but I keep thinking more and more about going back to Chicago. I wish I knew what God wants me to do."

"Maybe you don't know what God wants, because He wants you to take more time making a decision. When He's ready, you'll have your answer. You need to be patient."

The conversation continued as they neared the surgeon's office which was next door to the hospital. He came to Lincks once each week to see patients in the area. Since they were early, the ladies decided to see if Cindy was on duty.

"Dani, it's good to see you again, and Betty, I haven't seen you in far too long. This precious, little one must be Micah." Cindy had met them at the emergency room doors as they started into the building. "May I hold him?" She looked to Dani for permission. After receiving a nod, the doctor released the straps and removed the baby from the carrier. She cuddled him, and Micah grinned. Cindy laughed aloud. "He almost makes me want another baby," she declared, snuggling him close to her once more.

After a quick visit, it was time for Dani to make her way to the doctor's office. Betty had asked to take Micah with her to visit a friend in town while Dani saw the doctor. They decided to meet at Lucas' Deli. Betty pointed out the place as they came through town, so she would have no trouble finding the location after the appointment. She walked into the office, signed in, and was sent to x-ray. Then she was taken back to an exam room to wait for the doctor.

The surgeon was very prompt, and looked at the x-rays for a minute or more before turning to his patient. "Your arm is healing nicely. I think we can remove the cast to the middle of your forearm to give you more mobility. You'll need physical therapy to regain full use of your arm after we remove the cast."

"I can certainly do that." She was thrilled it was healing so well.

Leaving the doctor's office, Dani walked down the street and saw the Sheriff's office a block ahead of her. Without giving herself time to think about it, she headed that direction in hopes Garrett and Seth might be there.

She pushed open the door and walked into the cool reception area. As she spoke to the lady at the window, Seth came bounding down the hallway. "I saw you coming down the sidewalk," he said as he slammed into her body with a hug.

Garrett was right behind him. "Don't knock her off her feet, Seth." shaking his head as he walked up to her.

"Hi." They spoke at once and smiled.

Introductions were made around the station, as they made their way back to Garrett's office. "I see the doctor was able to remove part of the cast," he commented. Dani showed them both how much more she could do now. She mentioned the need for therapy, as well.

"Your mom and I are meeting at Lucas' Deli for lunch; do you have time to join us?" she asked after a bit.

"I think that's a great idea," Garrett told her. "One of the perks of being the boss, I can come and go pretty much as I please." Dani knew Garrett did not take advantage of his position, but she was glad he was able to get away to join them. "Do you want to drive or walk?"

Seth and Dani said "Walk," at the same time, so it was decided.

The weather was slightly cooler than usual, and there was just enough air moving to keep the humidity levels lower. No rain was in the forecast. The pace was leisurely as they each talked about their morning. With Garrett staying at the cottage, she did not always get to see him until evening, and she thought about how much she missed time with him, even if the rest of the family was there, too. Dani realized where her thoughts were taking her. She was thinking of Garrett and his family as her own, again. She could not let that continue. In a few weeks, she hoped to have the cast removed completely and could be back in Chicago. Her happy mood vanished.

"What's wrong?" he asked, leaning down toward her.

"Nothing's wrong."

"Something is. I felt your mood change a minute ago."

Am I that transparent, or is he that good? She was not sure. "I'm fine, really." Dani smiled back at him. "Seth, wait for us." The boy's presence allowed her to keep distance between herself and Garrett.

The deli was busy when they arrived. They spotted Betty in the corner with Lucas. He held his grandson, grinning as they approached the table.

"I hope you don't mind I'm holding Micah, Dani." Lucas blushed slightly.

"You never have to ask to hold him, Grandpa." She emphasized the name as she kissed him on the cheek.

"Yeah, enjoy holding him while you can, Lucas." Garrett looked at Dani.

"What are you talking about Garrett?" Lucas didn't understand.

"Ask Dani. She's talking about moving back to Chicago." Garrett continued to watch Dani, waiting for her to deny it.

"He's not right, is he, Dani? You surely aren't thinking about moving back. I just found family again. I don't want to lose you. Please say you're not thinking about leaving."

"I don't know what I am going to do, Lucas. I love it here, but at the same time, I can't continue to hurt Adam with our presence."

"So we all lose you to make Adam happier? That doesn't seem right, Darlin'."

Dani looked at Betty, silently asking for her help.

Betty turned toward the men with her hands on her hips. "She isn't going anywhere for a while. Both of you give her time to see what God wants her to do. He knows the right path for Dani and Micah. Now let's eat some lunch. I'm hungry."

"Come on, Lucas. I'll help you make the sandwiches." Garrett said.

As the men walked toward the kitchen, Lucas whispered to him. "I hope you have a plan to keep Dani here, Garrett. I don't think either of us wants to see her leave town, do we?"

Garrett grinned at his friend, but did not comment as they began making the sandwiches.

After a leisurely lunch, the men walked the ladies and the children to the car. Betty told Lucas goodbye while Garrett put the carrier in the car seat and made sure Seth was buckled up. When he turned, he caught Dani staring at him and grinned.

"Do you need me to buckle you in as well?" he teased.

"I think I can manage," she answered, flustered he had seen her. As she turned to open the passenger door, he stepped between the door and her.

"Tonight we are going to get to the bottom of your reason for the cold shoulder all of a sudden. You might as well be ready to tell me." He tapped his finger on her nose and opened the door from behind him, all the while looking into her eyes. "For now, you run home with Momma, little rabbit. The big, bad wolf isn't going to get you, yet."

<hr>

All afternoon, Dani was nervous about seeing Garrett tonight. She was so afraid he would see the truth when he looked at her. She was more attracted to the man than she wanted to admit, even to herself. As she sat thinking, Betty told her she was wanted on the phone.

"Dani, this is Cindy. I called to invite you to dinner tonight. Actually, Garrett has already accepted for both of you, but I wanted to ask you personally."

"Thanks. That sounds nice. Can we bring anything?"

"Not a thing, except those sweet boys of yours. We'll see you this evening."

When she told Betty about the change in dinner plans, Betty clapped her hands. "That works out perfectly. Lucas and I are going to dinner and a movie. I planned to cook for you all first, but this will be much nicer. Do you need help finding something to wear?"

Instead of avoiding Garrett all evening, she was going to spend the entire evening with him. At least, Cindy and her husband would be there.

———※———

Garrett stepped from the cruiser dressed in a t-shirt and jeans. The t-shirt fit snugly across his broad shoulders tapering to his hips where the jeans fit perfectly. *He just looks sexy.* Dani felt like a teenager, and she forced herself to turn around to keep from staring at him. She could not let herself get too attracted to him.

Betty was standing in the hallway watching her. She also could see Garrett coming up the drive. "He looks just as handsome out of uniform, doesn't he?" The question was made, not expecting an answer as she turned down the hallway with a grin on her face, causing the younger woman to grin also.

Dani was wearing a red sundress with matching red sandals. Garrett opened the door, while she was still standing at the window. His eyes went from her face to her toes and back.

"Wow. Did I have the wrong character earlier? You look good enough to devour, Red." Garrett's look told her just how much he appreciated the way she was dressed, and the comment was not lost on her either. She felt herself blush the color of her dress. By his hearty laugh, she knew he had received just the reaction he wanted.

Garrett declared himself officially off duty. He loaded the boys into his mom's car, since Lucas was picking Betty up for their date.

"Relax and have a good time tonight." Betty waved as she called out to them. Dani was not sure it was possible as tied up in knots as her emotions were at the moment.

━━━❀━━━

Mike and Cindy Guthrie had a cozy home in town, close to both the hospital and the fire station. As the family piled out of the door to greet them, Dani felt herself begin to relax. Garrett grabbed Micah from the back seat, showing him off to Mike. Cindy put her arm around Dani's waist and walked in the house with her while Seth and the boys took off for the backyard.

"Good to see the doctor removed part of your cast today. How's it healing?" Cindy turned to look at the woman beside her.

Dani told her what the doctor had said.

"I know a great therapist in town, when you're ready. Let's head outside. Everything is just about ready. The 'fire master' just needs to cook the meat." Cindy looked at Mike expectantly.

"I think she means me." He jumped up to put the meat on the grill. They had an enjoyable steak dinner around the outdoor dining table. While the children ran off to play, the adults moved to the living area. Mike and Cindy each took a chair, leaving the loveseat for Garrett and Dani.

As Garrett sat down, he took Dani's hand, pulling her gently down to the seat. Releasing her hand, he moved his arm to the back of the loveseat. He felt her body tensing before he leaned over to whisper "Relax," in her ear. He ran his hand under her hair and rubbed the back of her neck.

Mike had to ask her twice, when she started her new job.

"Oh, I'm sorry. Teachers begin in about two weeks. We report on Wednesday before Labor Day. I'm sure you know the students start the Tuesday after. I'm having second thoughts though and may be returning to Chicago."

Cindy had picked up the conversation. "Dani, you can't go back to Chicago. You already have a home here. You'll have Seth and David, our middle one, in your class. The school is small enough there's only one class per grade. The boys are already talking about you being their teacher. Why would you think about going back to that huge city?"

"It's just a crazy notion she has. We're not going to let her go," Garrett spoke up.

The conversation became more general until someone mentioned the weather. Mike bemoaned the lack of rain, worried about grass fires. There had already been three fires in the county, started by careless people tossing cigarettes from car windows.

"Labor Day is always a bad time with so many people cooking on outdoor grills," Mike stated.

David and Seth ran up to the group asking about dessert.

"I guess they're ready for cake," Cindy said, as she rose from her seat.

"I'll help you." Mike and Dani started to rise.

"Thanks, Mike," Garrett responded, placing a little pressure on her shoulder to keep her seated.

She turned to him whispering, "I should've helped her."

"Mike is certainly capable. Besides, I like having you next to me, and you would have definitely grabbed the chair if you could have. You've avoided me since we walked to the Deli this morning. What's wrong, Dani?" Garrett's voice took on such a soothing quality she wanted to melt into his arms.

Just then, Cindy and Mike walked outside with plates and a chocolate ice cream cake.

"To be continued later, Red," Garrett whispered close to her ear.

That's what I am afraid of.

Before they drove out of town, Seth was asleep and Dani's eyes were getting heavy. Garrett moved his hand under her hair, massaging her neck.

"I'm pretty sure bucket seats were invented by a father not wanting his daughter to get too close to the boyfriend. I miss the feel of you beside me." His voice was soft, as to not wake the boys.

"Garrett—"

His sharp intake of breath interrupted her. "Dani, call nine-one-one. Tell them the Henderson place is on fire and to send help." He was already heading down the drive toward the fire. "Do you think you can drive the car home? I don't want to worry about you and the boys." They both jumped out of the car. "I have to go. Get home safely, Red." He leaned down, and quickly kissed her lips, not waiting for her answer. He ran toward the fire.

Dani climbed into the driver's seat. She heard the wail of sirens as she backed out of the drive and started toward the house.

Please God, protect the couple living in this house; protect the firemen as they battle the fire, and please protect Garrett. Bring them all safely through this.

You know I love them all, Dani. I will be with them through everything.

She had not heard God's voice in quite a while. Truth was she knew He was there; she just had not taken the time to listen for Him. Parking the car, first she went and unlocked the front door. Then she carried Micah in his carrier to the sofa, and went back to get Seth. She was not sure if she could carry him or not.

As she undid his seatbelt and reached for him, car lights shone through the back window. Betty and Lucas were home. Lucas carried the boy to his bedroom and Betty helped get him undressed and into bed.

When they returned to the living room, Dani related what she knew about the fire. They had noticed the smoke driving home. Lucas walked to Betty, placing his thumb and finger under her chin. He kissed her soundly on the mouth. "I'll go see if Garrett needs a ride home."

Neither Dani nor Betty could think about sleeping. Micah began fussing, so they got him into his pajamas, fed him a bottle, and put him back to sleep.

"Want some tea?" Dani asked.

"Yes, please. It could be a long night," Betty replied.

Dani asked how their evening had been. Betty told her a little about the show and then asked about dinner at the Guthrie's. Dani shared the night's events.

"I'm glad you like Mike and Cindy. They're important to Garrett. I have a personal question, and you don't have to answer if you don't want to. When did you fall in love with Garrett?"

Dani almost dropped the glass she was holding. Did she love Garrett? She did not want to, but she knew it was true. Garrett was the man she had waited her whole life to meet. The Prince Charming her father said would find her one day. She did not have any idea how he felt about her though. Was it fair to even think about him, when she could be going back to Chicago?

"How can I be in love with Garrett? I just met him. I can't love him if I'm thinking about leaving. I don't want to hurt anyone."

Betty smiled at Dani. "We don't get to choose when we fall in love, dear. When it's the right person, it just happens. You need to let Garrett know you care about him. Give yourselves a chance before you think about leaving."

Dani looked at her. "I can't tell him how I feel, Betty. I don't want Garrett to pity me or be embarrassed for not feeling the same way."

"What makes you think he doesn't feel the same way?" Betty asked.

Dani did not know what to say, so she quickly changed the subject. "I think it's time I moved to the cottage and sent Garrett back home. I realized I could do things for myself tonight. I got Micah into the house just fine. I was able to help get him ready for bed. I was going to get Seth in the house when you and Lucas drove up."

Betty stopped her. "We noticed. I don't know which of us was more afraid you would hurt yourself, Lucas or me. Dani, you don't have a car. You don't know what kind of damage you would do to your arm, caring for Micah. I know you think you're ready to be on your own, but please give it some more time. You need to think about starting school, not worrying about where you're staying."

"That reminds me of something Cindy told me tonight. It concerns me a little. She said there was only one class per grade level at the school, and I would be teaching Seth and David, one of their sons. Do you think Seth will mind, if I decide to stay?"

"I don't think he'll be bothered at all. In fact, he has already thought about it, and knows how hard it will be to call you Miss McMichaels, after calling you Dani. Your biggest problem will be the fights he starts when a child says something about you. Seth loves you as much as I do, as much as we all do," Betty grinned.

Dani leaned over and gave her a hug. "I love you, too. Thank you." She and Betty yawned at the same time.

"If we are going to be awake in the morning when those boys get up, I think we better try to get some sleep, don't you?"

Just as Dani nodded her agreement, her cell phone rang. It was Garrett. He was staying with Mike at the fire to make sure all of the hot spots were out. No one was hurt, and the fire did not spread to the house. They were able to contain the fire to the out-buildings. "God was with us tonight, Dani," Garrett stated.

"He certainly was, Garrett. Can I do anything for you?"

"No, I'm good, but it's nice of you to ask. Let Mom know I sent Lucas home and I love her. I'll see you tomorrow. And Dani, I had a good time this evening."

"So did I. Goodnight, Garrett." She hung up the phone. She meant it; she had enjoyed the company of the Guthrie's, and the time spent with Garrett.

After relaying the conversation, Betty asked if Dani needed any help getting ready for bed.

"This is easy to get off, Betty. I'll be fine tonight. Thanks. I don't suppose you would let me take Micah into my room tonight?"

"Let's wait until in the morning. He'll sleep the night through, I'm sure. But in case he doesn't, I'd sleep with one ear listening for any problems. Start your independence tomorrow."

Dani gave her another hug and kissed her cheek. "This is from Garrett and me, both. Thank you for being so wonderful."

"You're easy to love, Dani McMichaels." They went off to their bedrooms to sleep as much as they could.

Chapter Thirteen

Despite the late night, Dani woke early, took a quick shower and dressed. She noticed her Bible on the nightstand, and remembered Garrett had exchanged his with hers, when he first moved to the cottage. She had not taken the time to read the book in several months. Sitting in the overstuffed chair in one corner of the bedroom, Garrett's scent wafted from the leather, and she felt like his arms encircled her. The book opened to one of her favorite chapters, Proverbs three, and she read verses five and six.

Trust in the Lord with all your heart and lean not on your own understanding. In all your ways acknowledge Him, and He will make your paths straight.

Dani contemplated the words. She thought about everything that had happened the last few weeks. "I know there was a reason You brought Ami and Adam into my life. Lucas is Micah's Grandfather; of course you wanted him to be a part of us. Even Garrett, Betty, and Seth must be part of your plan. But where do I fit in, God? Am I supposed to be teaching like I thought a few weeks ago, or do I need to return to Chicago?"

She wanted so badly to stay in Lincks, but what about Adam? Could she hurt him? And what about the feelings she had for Garrett? Could she leave knowing how she felt about him? Did he feel anything for her, as Betty had hinted? Her talk with God left her as confused as before.

Going to the kitchen to warm Micah's milk, she expected to hear him fussing any minute. Maybe Betty could sleep a little longer. Dani walked quietly into the sitting room to Micah's crib, changed his diaper, and picked him up. A slight pain radiated through her left arm. Shifting the weight more into her right arm, she took him with her to the living room.

"Micah, I didn't think this through very well. Where will I sit to feed you without help?" The sofa and chair would be too soft to get out of with the baby in her arm. She turned back to the dining room, and scooted the chair out with her foot. Then she remembered, she had forgotten the bottle. Again shifting Micah in her good arm, she walked to the kitchen. Garrett stood there watching her. *Where had he come from?*

Not saying anything, he tested the milk on his wrist and brought it to her. "Do you want me to take him now, or are you going to continue to strain your left arm?" Without waiting for an answer, he took Micah from her arm and carried him outside to the deck, knowing she would follow. She watched him sit on the loveseat and pat the seat next to him.

She sat down beside him, as he fed Micah. "When did you get in?" She asked drinking in his profile as he watched the baby suckle the bottle.

"About thirty minutes ago, just long enough to take a shower and walk over. I wanted to see you before I went to sleep."

"What would you have done if I had still been asleep?"

"Honestly? I would have probably stood there and watched you until I got caught."

Dani's heart leapt to her throat. She didn't know how to respond.

"Dani, look at me please. I—"

"Dad, you're home!" Seth came bounding out the door.

"This is beginning to get frustrating to say the least," He said quietly before turning to Seth. "Good morning, Son. How did you sleep?" he asked with a grin.

Seth bent down and kissed Micah's forehead and said, "I had a dream about a fire, but God took care of it. Everything was okay."

"God takes care of everything, doesn't he, Buddy?" Garrett placed Micah over his shoulder and patted until he burped.

"Good one, Micah," Seth determined.

The screen door opened and Betty stepped out in her housecoat and slippers. "Good morning, everyone. Garrett, its Wednesday. Are you fixing breakfast or would you prefer I do it, today? I'm sure you're tired."

"I'm cooking breakfast this morning." Dani jumped from the seat and started toward the kitchen. "You sit, and I'll bring both of you some coffee. Seth, do you want juice now or with breakfast?"

"With breakfast, please."

What was Garrett going to say before Seth came outside? Was he ready for her to leave? He had to be tired of staying away from his family and his beautiful home. What did he mean about his earlier statement, "watching her sleep?" She had to make changes as soon as possible. Her life was in turmoil.

God please show me the way to save everyone the embarrassment of asking me to leave.

I have plans for you, my child. I will lead if you will follow.

She stopped and listened to the voice. She knew it was meant for her alone. "Thank you, God," she whispered.

Dani made the pancake batter adding bananas and chocolate chips without thinking. "Well, my last meal will be a good one," she muttered to herself. She had forgotten to take Betty and Garrett their coffee. As she poured the hot liquid, she heard voices arguing. Both stopped talking and looked at her when she walked out the door. "I'm sorry. I didn't mean to interrupt," Dani apologized.

"You weren't interrupting, sweetheart. In a way, the conversation affects you as much as us. Let's talk about it at breakfast, okay?" Betty's response brought a frown from Garrett, but he remained quiet.

As Dani finished cooking the last of the pancakes, she called the family to the table. Each one stopped to wash their hands and then sat down. Garrett said grace and Dani passed the platter.

"Oh wow, Dad, Dani made them with bananas and chocolate chips. I didn't have to choose." Seth bit into his, not waiting for the butter or syrup.

"Are you trying to take over Wednesday breakfast, showing me up?" Garrett had leaned over to ask the question, grinning at her.

She saw the grin and knew he was teasing her. "Maybe Lucas will give me a job in his deli." Dani shot back, but that only brought another frown from Garrett.

"Sorry, Mom has already decided to take that job, haven't you, Mom?" he stated pulling his gaze from Dani to his mother.

"Dani, Lucas asked me to marry him last night. He also talked about the two of us working together to expand the Deli into a restaurant. The marriage proposal didn't come with the job attached, Garrett. Lucas asked me to marry him because he loves me. It took him long enough to get up the courage, but he finally asked." She looked directly at him and then over to Dani. "I accepted. We want to get married soon, but that presents a problem. I had thought I would offer to keep Micah for you while you were at school, but now..."

"Oh Betty, please don't worry. I'll find someone to watch him. I would have to leave him with a sitter, no matter what I'm doing, or where I am. Please don't let us interfere with your plans." She hoped her voice sounded more confident than she felt. "I love both of you, and I'm thrilled he finally came to his senses," she added.

Garrett folded his napkin, pushed his chair back from the table, and announced, "I need sleep." He kissed his son on the head, his mother on the cheek, and walked by Dani without saying a word.

"Did I say something to upset him? Doesn't he want you to marry Lucas, Betty?" she asked.

"It's not that. He loves Lucas like a father. He's concerned about the restaurant. He thinks I'll overdo things. Seth, if you are through eating, will you check on Micah for us, please?" Betty waited for him to take his plate to the kitchen before finishing. "You see, dear, I have a heart condition that flares up if I get overly tired or exerted. Garrett doesn't think I know my limitations and will work too hard. But I know when to rest. I plan to see my grandchildren married with children of their own. I'm not through on this earth yet, not by a long shot." She grinned at Dani and patted her hand. "Now let's see what those boys are up to, shall we?"

Chapter Fourteen

Teachers reported to school in six days. *Where has this summer gone? I still can't decide if I should stay in Lincks. God, I need some help. If I'm going to stay here, I have to find a sitter for Micah. Wherever I go, I need to find a car. What I really need is Your direction.* She had uttered the prayer so many times; God was probably tired of hearing it. Just then her cell phone rang. It was a local call, but not a number she recognized. "This is Dani."

"Uh, Dani, it's Adam. I hope it's not too early to call, but the Lord has been laying this on my heart for days now, and I can't stop thinking about it."

"Well, Adam, if the Lord is telling you to do something, you'd better listen. How can I help you?"

"God keeps telling me over and over, I need to give you Ami's vehicle." The pause was so long, Adam asked if she was still there.

"Adam, that's incredible of you, but I can't just take Ami's car. Are you sure you even want to part with it?"

"Yes, it was too big for Ami. She didn't like driving a Crossover; she liked her old compact. I should've traded it, when she told me, instead of telling her she'd get used to it."

Dani hesitated just a second before asking, "Would you have time to drive over to Garrett's house and pick me up? I would like to drive it myself before I make you a proposition." An hour later, Dani and Adam had made a deal for the car. She could not accept it as a gift. This way it was an answer to both of their prayers. She felt guilty because he would not let her give him nearly the value of the Crossover, but he did accept some payment. While they were together, Dani wanted to discuss his feelings and her uncertainty about staying in Lincks. He was so quiet; she just did not feel right bringing up the hurtful subject. *God has taken care of the car. I just need to be patient and wait for more answers.*

Driving through town, Dani decided to stop and see Cindy. Hopefully the doctor could suggest someone to care for her son. She spotted her friend talking to a couple outside an exam room. A moment later, Cindy walked up to join her.

"This is a pleasant surprise. What brings you to town?" Cindy asked, giving Dani a quick hug.

Dani explained about the new vehicle and the need to find a sitter.

"Hopefully this means you plan to stay in town. The woman who watches the boys for us was just saying she'd love to have another baby in the house. Mrs. Franklin only keeps our children and doesn't have them every day, unless we're both on call at the same time. She is fabulous with the boys, and lives two doors from the school. Let me give you her address and phone number."

Leaving the hospital, Dani decided to stop by Mrs. Franklin's rather than call. Anyone babysitting children should not mind someone dropping in. She left the woman's home, knowing Micah would be in good hands. God certainly seemed to be opening doors for her to stay in town. She was more confused than ever.

Driving by the town square, she noticed a police car following her. Suddenly the lights came on and an order to pull over came from the patrolman. She pulled into an available parking space. Garrett blocked her car with his and got out of the vehicle. He walked to the front door, opening it before she had a chance to say anything.

"Get out of the car, Ma'am." He was acting as if she'd done something criminal.

"Garrett, what's wrong?" she asked, stepping out of the car.

Dani gasped at the gruffness in his voice when he finally answered, "I'm counting to ten before I decide what I am going to do with you, Miss McMichaels." He hadn't removed his sunglasses and her reflection stared back at her. By now, Garrett had leaned against the car with his hands on either side of her, effectively pinning her to it. "What do you think you are doing driving, and why do you have Ami's car?"

Dani resented the tone the sheriff used with her and stood a little taller. The green flecks appeared in her eyes as she shot back at him, "I have a driver's license, Sheriff Austin, and I'm quite capable of driving. I have Ami's car, because Adam sold it to me this morning. Do you have a problem with that?" She cocked her head to one side, daring him to say anything.

"The problem I have is your control of the vehicle, Ma'am," emphasizing the last word. "With your arm in that cast, you couldn't control the car effectively, if you were to have trouble. Now give me the keys and get in the patrol car. I'll take you home."

"And if I don't sheriff, what are you going to do, arrest me?"

"Don't tempt me, Danielle McMichaels, don't tempt me." He took hold of her right arm at the elbow applying enough pressure to move her toward his cruiser.

"Better lock her up, Garrett." Mike was driving by and hollered out the window without stopping. He laughed, as he drove on.

"Now see what you have done." Dani said, throwing the words up at him.

"Lady, you brought this on all by yourself when you pulled this hair-brained stunt."

She pulled away from him and stomped her foot. "In case you have forgotten, you were the one who told me to drive home the other night, remember?"

Garrett swung around in front of her grabbing both arms just below the shoulders. He answered through gritted teeth, "That was an emergency. All I could do was pray you could get home okay. I couldn't worry about you and the boys and help with the fire at the same time. Now get in the car." He jerked the door open on the squad car. He slammed the door after he knew she was seated and walked to the driver's side.

"You still haven't given me the keys," he growled as he held his hand out flat.

Dani dropped the keys in his hand and looked out the window with tears forming in her eyes. Why was he acting this way? As she tried to become more independent, he stopped her at every turn. She had lived twenty-five years without his help. The trip home was made without a word.

As they pulled into the drive, Dani released her seatbelt and jumped quickly from the car, determined to get away from him. Unfortunately, he was faster. He grabbed her arm and swung her back toward him, knocking her into his chest where his arms locked around her like a vice grip. One arm loosened long enough for him to reach up and to grab her chin making her look up at him.

His eyes were no longer covered by the glasses, but she still could not read his expression. He looked down at her lips, as she wet them with her tongue. He groaned and dipped his head to capture her mouth in an embrace meant to punish. But as he heard her moan, Garrett softened the kiss, savoring her taste. He molded her body closer to his, and kissed her a second time. He raised his head, looking first at her lips and then to her eyes. Dani could only stare back at him.

As Garrett opened his mouth to say something, his cell phone went off. He pulled it from his belt, still looking into her eyes. "Austin" was the clipped response. He listened to the other end and said "I'll be right there." Ending the call, he said, "Dani, I—"

She did not wait for him to finish his sentence, but pulled from his grasp. Dani turned and ran into the house going straight into the bedroom in tears.

Betty stood in the living room, and watched Garrett leave after he knew Dani was safely in the house. Having watched the whole scene, she smiled to herself and walked into her room to check on Micah.

Chapter Fifteen

Dani's vehicle was in the driveway the next morning. She had not seen or heard from the sheriff. She stood staring at the car, thinking about how angry Garrett acted yesterday and then how he kissed her. *What made him so upset? Those kisses didn't end in anger though.*

Betty walked up behind her while she stood there. "Garrett called me early this morning. He said he sent your car to the house with Owen. He left you a note inside." Betty smiled as Dani turned to look at her friend. She nodded toward the car, encouraging her to go get it.

She opened the driver door to find an envelope lying in the seat. The envelope was not sealed as she took the paper out to read.

Dani, I have to apologize for the way I handled the situation yesterday. I can't explain the emotions I felt when I saw you driving a car. The thought of you getting hurt again made me crazy, I guess. I kept the keys. I'll give them back after your cast is removed. We need to talk.

He had not signed the note or mentioned the kisses. The note did not explain much other than the fact he was sorry. *Is he sorry about the way he acted or about the kisses or both? I agree; we do need to talk.*

Over lunch, Dani told Betty about Mrs. Franklin and the plan for her to keep Micah.

"Agnes and I sing together in the church choir. We've been friends for years. I don't know why I didn't think of her days ago. She's wonderful with children. She teaches Sunday school for the three-to-four-year-old class. Anyone able to teach that age can certainly handle a baby," Betty commented.

The endorsement from both Betty and Cindy was comforting to Dani. She was nervous enough about the job in the first place. Not worrying about Micah would help a lot. Now, she just had to decide if she wanted to stay in town or not. After last evening, Dani was not sure she was even welcome.

"You know, Betty; I haven't even seen the school where I'll be working. I only talked to the superintendent over the phone when I interviewed for the position."

"Let's go see Jacob then. It's time you met him and see the classroom. It might help you to make a decision about staying in Lincks as well."

As Dani walked with Betty and the boys through the halls of the administration offices, she thought about the preschool where she had been the director. With her degrees, the owner of the school said he had been thrilled to have her. Having had classroom experience would have been helpful for a position at that level, but she learned quickly, and the staff loved her, as she loved each of them.

The only problems were with the parents. Many felt the director was too inexperienced to be in charge of the school, and did not mind expressing their opinions. As any good administrator, Dani had them laughing and singing her praises by the time they left their first meeting. Teaching in a classroom was going to present a whole new set of challenges, but no one would know she was nervous about the position.

If God has provided this classroom for me, I'll do the best job possible to make sure the students thrive.

"Hi. I'm Dani McMichaels, the new second grade teacher. I was wondering if Mr. Chambers might be available to visit with me for a few minutes," she explained to the receptionist. As the woman dialed the man's office, Dani stepped back to look at the walls in the area. Portraits hung honoring past Superintendents and other men and women of distinction. Before she scanned the entire gallery, she heard shoes click on the tile floors. A gentleman walked toward her with his hand extended.

"Miss McMichaels, it's so good to finally meet you. I'm sorry your arrival to Lincks has been encumbered, should we say? I hope your arm is healing nicely."

Does everyone in town know what happened to me? But he seemed to be genuinely concerned about her well-being and she appreciated it.

The superintendent continued. "I was going to call you sooner, but I haven't had an opportunity to do so, yet. The last three weeks have been a whirlwind of activity in my office. Do you have a minute to discuss what's been happening?

"Oh, Betty, I'm so sorry I just noticed you sitting there. Are you here to see me, also?"

"Actually, Jacob, Dani is staying with Seth and me at Garrett's while she recuperates. I just brought her in to meet you and see her classroom, since she isn't able to drive yet with her cast. Dani, why don't Seth and I take Micah to Lucas' and wait for you there? I think Seth could eat an ice cream cone, and I'm sure Lucas would like to see the boys."

"Thank you, Betty. I shouldn't be too long." Dani replied. It seemed Betty and Mr. Chambers were friends, also. She had always heard that people in small towns knew everyone and their business.

Mr. Chambers showed her the way back to his office. Inside, he removed a box from the chair and invited her to have a seat.

"I'm so glad you stopped by. We have quite a bit to discuss." Jacob Chambers smiled at her across the desk, studying her as he talked.

"Since we only visited over the phone, I thought it might be a good idea to actually meet in person and see my classroom if it's possible." Dani returned his smile as he began to speak, again.

"Actually your classroom is one of the very things we need to chat about. Mrs. Thornsby, the teacher who was leaving when her husband received the transfer, has asked to return to her second grade position. Turns out they weren't at all happy in the big city and have moved back home."

"Oh." Dani gasped. *Did I just lose my job before I started? Maybe this is God's way of tell me I should move back to Chicago.*

"Now, before you get upset, and before I can give her an answer, I want to offer you a different challenge. The district would like to offer you the position of Director of Early Childhood for Lincks Schools." Jacob smiled.

"I wasn't aware you have an early childhood program in this district, other than Kindergarten, of course." Dani was surprised about the announcement.

"Miss McMichaels, may I call you Dani? At her nod, he continued. "Dani, we didn't have a program for our three and four year olds until a few days ago. We just received a very generous anonymous donation stipulated to be spent on creating the new classes for our younger students. Of course, the program will have to be built from the ground up. It will be quite the undertaking until it's established."

"Surely, there are better qualified people in the district than me, Mr. Chambers." Just the idea had Dani's heart racing.

"Please call me Jacob and let me assure you your name has been discussed with the Board in detail already. I mean it in a very good way, of course. You are, by far, the best qualified for the position with a Master's in Elementary Education and a Certificate in Administration. Combined with your minor in

Business Administration, it makes you highly desirable for this new program. You do possess those degrees, correct?"

"I do. I earned them at the University of Illinois." Dani assured him.

"That was the information we received. Before you were officially nominated for the position, a committee talked to members of the staff at your previous employment. We don't hire just anyone qualified. We only want the best for Lincks' schools. Ours is not a large district, and this will be a very important addition to our town.

"I'm sure you're aware of the studies, showing the importance of early childhood education. Not everyone is qualified to take on the commitment this will require to make it a success. We're very confident you're the perfect person for the position. So, do you need some time to think about this, or are you ready to jump in with both feet and make this program your own?" Mr. Chambers was a very smooth talker. He had certainly charmed her.

"Are you sure the board wouldn't like to meet with me first?" she asked.

"They would be happy to if you request it, but they've already approved the hiring. So what do you think?"

"Mr. Chambers, uh, Jacob, I need to pray about this. Part of my reason for coming to see you today was to tell you I might not be staying in Lincks, after all. Because of events in my life lately, I'm considering a return to Chicago. Can you give me a day or two, before I give you my answer?"

"Of course, of course, take all the time you need, as long as your answer is yes. We need you in Lincks, Dani." Jacob flashed a big grin and walked around the desk to shake hands. "I know this is a big decision, so by all means discuss it with God. I should tell you though, He and I have already talked about it, and you have His vote hands down. This position was meant to be yours."

"Thank you, Jacob. I'll call you soon with my decision." Dani left the building in a daze.

Am I ready for this much responsibility? Would the staff and residents of Lincks be as accepting of me as Jacob thinks they will? I need to talk with Garrett about this.

Then she remembered he was out of town. Besides she was still angry with him for taking the keys to her car. It would be far better to discuss this with Betty and Lucas. They could help her sort through her feelings about the decision. The idea of going to Chicago seemed much more difficult with Mr. Chambers' offer.

She was completely unaware of her surroundings as she walked to the Deli, her mind deep in thought. As she walked through the door, Seth lunged at her. He grabbed her around the waist and squeezed.

"You were gone a long time; I missed you," he giggled because he startled her.

Grinning, she returned the hug, and wrapped her arm around his shoulders. "I missed you too, Sweetheart. Where is Grandma and Micah?"

"They're in the back with Lucas. Did you know he is going to be my new Grandpa? Isn't that awesome?" Seth jumped from foot to foot with excitement.

Dani smiled at him and pulled him close. "Did you know you and Micah will both be his Grandsons?"

"Wow! Grandma, Micah and I are going to be related. I can teach him everything I know just like Mark and David teach Johnny," he hollered, as he ran to the back of the deli.

Betty stepped out of the kitchen to greet Dani. "I must have missed part of your conversation." Betty's grin lingered as they embraced. "Come and tell us how the meeting went."

After greeting Lucas with a hug and a kiss, Dani sat down at the table and proceeded to tell them what had happened.

"So what do you think you want to do?" Lucas asked.

"I told him I had to pray about it. Mr. Chambers, Jacob, said God had already voted for me, but I'd like to hear it for myself. I'm not sure I'm qualified, or if I can handle that much responsibility. Then, there's still the problem of Adam and his feelings."

"Dani, they wouldn't offer you the position if they didn't think you were capable of handling it." Betty almost scolded her.

"Does that mean you won't be my teacher?" Seth had been very quiet through the entire conversation.

"I might not, buddy. Would it make you sad?"

He replied, "Yeah, kind of, but Mrs. Thornsby is nice, too. She's just not as pretty as you are, Dani."

"And that's why he will be President, someday." Dani laughed, and the others joined her.

Chapter Sixteen

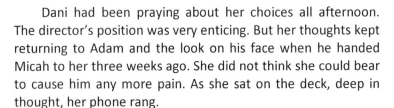

Dani had been praying about her choices all afternoon. The director's position was very enticing. But her thoughts kept returning to Adam and the look on his face when he handed Micah to her three weeks ago. She did not think she could bear to cause him any more pain. As she sat on the deck, deep in thought, her phone rang.

"Adam, I was thinking about you—"

"I hear you're talking about leaving because of me." His voice was harsh, cutting her off before she could say anything more. "Dani, my feelings have nothing to do with the life you have planned for you and your son. I couldn't stand the burden of thinking you left because of me. Knowing Micah is this close is probably the only thing keeping me sane at this point. I know I can't be around him right now, but you have to know I love your baby. I would never do anything more to hurt either of you. Micah isn't my son. I knew it all along, but I hope one day you'll forgive me enough to let me see him occasionally and watch him grow up. Please don't take that away from me. You belong in Lincks, not for me, but for yourself and for Micah. Tell me you aren't going to move back to Chicago."

Dani didn't speak for several seconds. "I don't know what to say, Adam. I never expected this. I honestly don't know what God wants me to do, but your call means a lot to me. I know God wants you to be a part of Micah's life. I can't promise you I'll stay in town, but we'll stay in touch. I want Micah to know his family in Lincks. I'll talk to you in a day or two, okay?"

"Okay, Dani. I know you have to make the best decision for you and your son. Take care." The call ended before she could say anything further.

I wonder how Adam even knew about my indecision to stay in Lincks. Garrett or Lucas must have told him. I have even more to pray about now.

⁂

Praying and reading her Bible hadn't given Dani any clearer answers, until she came across First Corinthians, chapter seven, verse twenty-four. The verse spoke to her.

Brothers, each man as responsible to God, should remain in the situation God called him to.

Two years ago, Dani had felt the calling of the Lord to the preschool. It was the right place for her to be then.

This must be why He brought me to Lincks, not to teach second grade, but to start basically the same type of program here. But what about Adam? I think he was sincere about the things he said. I feel comfortable with the idea God wants Micah to be a part of Adam's life. God must be leading me to stay in Lincks.

Lucas had been invited to eat dinner with them and was visiting with Betty when Dani walked into the room. She told them both the decision she made.

"It's a good thing you listened to God, Dani. Otherwise Garrett and I wasted the town's money."

"What are you talking about Lucas?"

"Garrett and I were both on the school board. I'm surprised you didn't see our mug shots hanging in the hallways of the Administrative Center. We've already resigned though, so there wouldn't be any conflict of interest. We'll have to call an emergency vote of the people to elect two new board members."

"You knew about this before I told you?"

"Just for a few days Dani, not long." Lucas realized he should not have said anything, but Dani was bound to find out. It did not really matter; no one opposed hiring her.

Confused about her feelings again, Dani told them she was going to take a walk along the shore. She wanted to think without distractions. The night was quiet with only the chirping of crickets to keep her company.

She wondered why someone had not told her this earlier. After talking about teaching, somebody should have mentioned Garrett and Lucas served on the school board. It did not make any difference she supposed, but she wondered if that was why her name was brought forward. Maybe she should not take the position. Just when she thought God had given her the answer, this came up. Dani was back to questioning everything. *It's time like this I miss you, Mom.*

Dani was so engrossed in what she was thinking that she did not hear the noise until something touched her arm. Swinging at whatever was behind her, she heard and felt the thud at the same time. It was a solid object, a big solid object. Garrett stood there, catching his breath, trying not to laugh.

"You scared the daylights out of me, Garrett Austin."

"I'm so sorry, Dani. For what it's worth, I'm sure I'll have a bruise in the morning."

"Did I hurt you?" Her voice changed instantly from censure to concern. She reached out to touch the area she smacked with her cast. "I didn't know it was you. Are you sure you're not hurt?"

"Hmm, I could be, you know. I could be so hurt I require CPR. Would you give me CPR?" Garrett whispered as he leaned his forehead against hers.

Dani was afraid she might be the one needing the CPR. "When did you get home?"

"Changing the subject, are we? I got in about an hour ago. I had some paperwork to finish before I came home. Lucas told me he let the board thing slip. Are you angry with us?"

Dani looked up at Garrett. The moon was shining on his face creating sharp planes. Her mind filled with thoughts of him as she gazed at his chiseled good looks.

"Earth to Dani." he teased, bringing her back into focus.

"Oh. No, I'm not angry, just confused. I received a phone call from Adam. I'm sure you or Lucas must have talked to him. Then, I thought God had led me to take this position. That was before Lucas told me about the two of you being on the School Board. Garrett, if I take the job now, it'll look like a set-up."

"Dani, everyone knows you're qualified for this position. Believe me, when I tell you as a School Board member, we wouldn't hire just anyone. We want only the best person qualified."

Dani giggled.

"Did I say something funny?"

"Jacob Chambers said almost exactly the same thing earlier. Did your board rehearse that line?" The grin told him she was teasing.

"Do you remember me telling you about the conversation I had with your friend, Amanda Black? Well, as much as that woman scares me, and you know not much scares me as Sheriff of Lincks County, I called her after I knew who you were and why you were here."

"You investigated me?" She raised an eyebrow.

"I couldn't let a stranger in my house to live with my family unless I knew it was safe. I have a reputation to keep, woman. Anyway, I talked to Amanda about you. I had the name of the school from your fingerprints we received after the accident. I talked to several teachers and some of the parents, and not just happy parents. Your old secretary was very helpful in giving me a cross section of parents to talk to. Every single person told me the same thing. You're a woman of integrity, honesty and professionalism. You left a real fan club in Chicago, Miss McMichaels."

"Really?" Dani grinned, flattered by the compliment.

"Yes, really." Garrett tapped her on the end of her nose. "Didn't you wonder why Mike, of all people brought up the subject of school the night we had dinner with them? Mike, Jolene and Frank Warner are the other members of the school board. Each one formed their own opinion of you. Except for

Frank, of course, he only knows you by reputation. You're going to accept this position, aren't you, Dani?"

She looked out across the water for a moment. "You know, I'm not sure if I should whack you with my cast again for not telling me all this before, or kiss you for all the nice things you just said about me."

Before she could say anything more, Garrett turned her toward him and stated "I vote for kissing me." She laughed, stretching on tiptoes to brush her lips across his cheek.

His hands spanned her waist to keep her close as he said, "Why, Miss McMichaels if that's the best you can do, I may have to change my vote. I thought you were good at persuading people to see things your way."

Dani accepted the challenge and wrapped her right arm around his neck. "Sheriff Austin, most of my parents are willing to meet me halfway, but if you can't see fit to do so, I guess I'll have to be a little more persuasive." She grinned at him as she snuggled closer and kissed his lips. Tipping her head back, she asked, "Is this persuading you yet?"

Garrett replied "Nope," and pretended to yawn.

Dani frowned and commented, "It's not easy, when we're not seeing things eye to eye, you know."

He picked her up by the waist and carried her to the step of the deck. "How's this?" he asked with his hands still holding her.

"Hmm, better," she stated snuggling her face into his neck, planting feathery kisses as she moved toward his cheek and finally his mouth. She moved her lips over his, willing him to respond. When he still resisted, she ran her tongue across his lips. Finally she heard a deep moan from Garrett as he wrapped his arms tighter around her body, pulling her toward him. At the same time, he started to return the kiss, parting her lips to taste the sweetness she offered. Breathless, she pulled away from him enough to look into his eyes.

"I think I'm beginning to see things your way," he said with a wry grin on his face.

Dani felt like she was drowning and took the only way out she could think of. She laid her cheek against his and turning toward his ear, nipped it.

Garrett pulled away in surprise asking, "Why did you bite me?"

"Because you took away my car keys. Besides it was only a little nip," she laughed and started to go up the steps to the house.

"Oh no, you don't," he said as he grabbed at her arm.

She was quicker than he was as she stepped off the deck onto the soft grass instead. "Garrett, I'm sorry, really. That wasn't nice." The whole time she was apologizing she was backing away as he advanced toward her rubbing his ear at the same time. She giggled and turned to run away from him, but his legs were too long.

As he reached her, the screen door opened and Lucas stepped onto the deck. "Garrett, you're going to have to marry that girl, so the rest of us can get some peace and quiet. I'm too old to be laughing this hard."

Both of them realized they had an audience the whole time. They looked at each other and Garrett spoke first. Suddenly, his face was serious. "Do you want to marry me, Dani?"

Dani's smile faded, and she could no longer deny her feelings for this man. She wanted nothing more than to marry Garrett Austin. She grinned at him and meekly answered, "If that's a proposal, yes, I want to marry you."

Garrett wrapped his hands around her waist as he twirled her around, and set her on her feet in front of him. As he leaned his head in to kiss her, his cell phone rang. He knew the sound of the ring meant a fire somewhere. "I have to go."

He kissed her lips quickly and whispered he would be back as soon as possible. He bounded across the area between the house and the cottage to his squad car. He was gone before Dani could wave goodbye.

She looked at the people standing on the deck and walked up to join them. "I'm not sure what just happened. I told the man I wanted to marry him when he has never even said he loves me. What's wrong with me?"

She looked so forlorn; Betty reached over and hugged her. "It's going to be just fine, Dani. He'll be back soon enough."

Garrett was gone for two days. The fire had consumed more than ten thousand acres, before they were able to get it under control. Three homes had been destroyed, but no lives were lost. He looked exhausted when he walked through the back door. Dani sat at the dining room table feeding Micah as he walked right up to her.

Before she had the opportunity to say anything he said, "I did ask you to marry me right?" She nodded. "And you did accept, didn't you?" She grinned and nodded, once more. "Just wanted to make sure I wasn't dreaming. I have to take a shower." He bent down and kissed Dani with more passion than she expected.

He started to leave the house. Before the door closed, she heard him walk back into the room. He placed a hand on either side of her face and said, "I love you. I'll tell you again when I've slept long enough to say it properly. We're going to dinner tonight, and I don't want any more interruptions." He kissed her once more and went back out the door. He looked so tired, Dani was not sure if Garrett would even remember talking to her this morning.

Chapter Seventeen

Labor Day was four days away. Betty had already told Dani about the town picnic the merchants of Lincks provided every year. They had carnival rides, games, and activities for the entire family. Lucas and Garrett always manned the grills while other men and women served side dishes and desserts.

The ladies and boys drove into Lincks, leaving Garrett to sleep while they helped Lucas with as many preparations as they could. Dani was eager to help since she did not have a classroom to get ready. After spending the morning working with Jacob Chambers, she walked to the deli with a plan in mind.

Dani moved to stand in front of Betty and Lucas. "I have a wonderful idea. Everyone knows about your engagement and since most of the town will be there anyway, you two should get married Labor Day afternoon on the square. What do you say?"

Lucas' face lit up and he threw his hands into the air. "What a great idea. Why didn't we think of that?"

Betty looked from Lucas to Dani. "We've talked about a small wedding. How could I possibly get a wedding together in four days?" She reached for the nearest chair.

"You just tell me you want to get married Labor Day, and I'll prepare whatever you need. What have you planned?" Dani coaxed her.

"I have to get a dress, and Dani, will you stand up with me? Lucas, are you going to want Garrett to be your best man?

I'd like to have a small cake to cut. Flowers and decorations will already be in place. We have to ask Reverend Jenkins to make sure he's available to do the ceremony. I can't think of anything else."

"Simple enough," Dani stated. "Lucas, will you watch the boys? We're going shopping."

Two places in town sold the type of dresses Betty had in mind. They walked in the first store and found exactly what she wanted in fifteen minutes. The owner was more than happy to have the alterations finished for them by Labor Day. They even found shoes to match.

The two ladies walked to the bakery and ordered the cake Betty chose. Then they headed back to the deli. Dani told the couple they should go to the courthouse. "Without a license, you can't get married, and they'll be closed soon. Seth and I'll watch the store while you're gone."

Just as she finished waiting on a customer, Dani's cell phone rang.

"Where are you?" Garrett asked.

"Well, hello to you, too. I'm at the deli. We're having a wedding, Garrett."

"We're what?" Garrett sounded like he was choking, making Dani grin even bigger.

"Not you and I, silly, your mom and Lucas are getting married Labor Day while everyone is here for the party. They're so excited. I sent them to the courthouse. Garrett, we get to stand up with them. Betty and I already purchased our dresses. You and Lucas are going to wear suits, so you don't have to be fitted for a tux. We ordered the cake earlier, and Betty is going to use the decorations from the Labor Day festivities. They're going to talk to Reverend Jenkins this evening. Everything will be just beautiful, and since everyone already knows them, it'll be like a huge reception after the ceremony. Why haven't you said anything? Are you upset?"

"I'm not upset. A certain little gal I know has been doing all the talking. All I want is their happiness. I talked to Lucas about my concerns. He and Mom had already discussed them. He'll take good care of her. So, when are you coming home?"

"Well, since I don't have a car and we're minding the deli, we'll have to wait for Betty to come back, and we'll be home when she's ready."

"I'll be there in thirty minutes." Garrett hung up.

The sheriff arrived a few minutes after Betty and Lucas.

"Mom, I hope you don't mind keeping Micah, Seth is spending the night at the Guthrie's. Seth, I packed your things. Dani and I'll drop you off on our way back to the house."

"Yay thanks, Dad. I haven't been over there in ages. They might not even remember me," he teased.

"Tell everyone goodbye and get in the car, smarty pants." Garrett grinned at his son.

Seth laughed and gave everyone a hug. He was in the car and buckled up by the time Garrett and Dani stepped outside.

She turned and cocked her head at him. He was driving her car. "I thought you might like to ride in something besides a police car," he said, grinning sheepishly. "We don't want people thinking the new early childhood director is in trouble with the law already, do we?" As he asked the question, he opened the passenger door for her.

They took Seth to the Guthrie's and headed toward Garrett's house.

Where are we going tonight, Garrett?" Dani was excited, looking forward to spending the time with him. She was not alone with Garrett too often and certainly not for an extended length of time.

"It's a surprise. The red sundress you wore to Mike and Cindy's will be just fine," he said waggling his eyebrows with a grin on his face. He dropped her off at the house with a warning to be ready in one hour, or he was taking her like she was.

She hurried inside. Looking through the closet, she chose a print dress in oranges, yellows, and reds. The bodice was peasant style with a long flowing skirt, making it easy to pull on over the cast. The red sandals matched the dress also. She was ready in fifty-five minutes.

She thumbed through a magazine, as she waited for him. It had been an hour and ten minutes. Garrett was never late for anything. Dani decided to walk down to the cottage to make sure everything was okay. Both her car and the cruiser were in the drive, meaning he had not been called out.

Dani knocked lightly and did not hear anything. The door was unlocked, so she went in. Walking through the house, everything looked alright. Passing by the bedroom, she saw him sprawled out on the bed sound asleep. He had not slept much at all the last few days. She did not have the heart to wake him. Dani walked over to her grandmother's old rocker and sat down to watch him sleep. *Marriage to Garrett Austin will be anything, but quiet, and moments like this won't come often.* Waiting for him to wake would be fine.

Sometime during the evening, Dani fell asleep. She stirred as a kiss brushed her lips. "Hmm, Prince Charming." she said sleepily. Then her eyes popped open. "You did kiss me in the hospital, didn't you? I thought I was dreaming."

Garrett blushed; something he seldom did, "It was your fault. You looked so beautiful with your hair spread out all over the pillow and your lips looking so kissable. I couldn't resist you from the first time I saw you, Danielle McMichaels. You captured my heart without opening your eyes."

Dani stood to kiss the man she loved. As Garrett deepened the kiss, he molded her body to his.

Garrett pulled away first. "We have to get out of here, now, or I'll never let you leave."

Dani smiled; a dimple showing in each cheek. "Do you want me to leave?"

He growled, the noise coming from deep in his chest. "We're both leaving." Garrett grabbed two sweatshirts from the closet and the blanket from the bed. "Let's go watch the sunrise since we missed dinner."

They stopped at an all-night gas station and Garrett went inside. He came back with a sack and two large coffees. He put the sack in the back seat and handed her one of the coffees. Then he drove to the top of a hill overlooking a big valley.

"We should have just enough time to find our seats before the headlights go out," he told her. "Grab the sweatshirts and the blanket. I'll bring the coffee and snacks." After they had everything in their arms, Garrett reached in and turned off the motor. The lights gave them about one minute to scamper up to the rock ledge and find a place to sit.

The early morning air had a slight chill to it, crisp, but not cold. Dani handed one of the sweatshirts to Garrett, and she pulled on the other one. It was big enough to come almost to her knees.

"Sit down and wrap the blanket around your legs. You're going to get cold quickly with your dress on. You look beautiful by the way, Dani." The look in his eyes caressed her.

Garrett turned back to begin his task. "If you'll watch the drinks so they don't spill, I'll prepare your pastry. I saw this once on one of those chick flicks Mom was watching. The guy got the girl, by the way. Had to be a good dessert, I figured."

She saw his grin in the pre-dawn light. Dani wrapped one side of the blanket around her legs as she sat on the other side.

Soon Garrett held his creation out to her in his right hand as he placed his left hand over his right arm. "Just like the fancy waiters; nothing, but the best for my girl."

Dani's heart fluttered. She loved the sound of those words. She took the pastry offered and giggled. It was a sponge cake with strawberry jam on top. As Garrett sat down beside her, she thanked him for the dessert. They ate in comfortable silence while looking over the horizon.

"This isn't quite the evening I had pictured for us, Dani." Garrett stated. "I had reservations for a candle light dinner at a nice restaurant. I'm sorry I fell asleep."

Dani turned slightly toward him resting on her right hand. "I wouldn't change a thing about tonight. I've loved every minute of it. Just being with you is enough for me."

Garrett kissed her quickly and then got onto one knee. "I wanted this to be a romantic evening for you, but I can't wait any longer. I love you, Danielle McMichaels. I've loved you since the moment I first saw you. I also love your son. I want to spend the rest of my life with both of you. Will you do me the honor of becoming my wife?" He held an open box out to her. It was just light enough to make out a beautiful diamond ring with a filigree band.

"I will become your wife, Garrett Austin, any time, any place. I fell in love with you when you kissed me in the hospital."

Garrett sat beside her once more and pulled her onto his lap. Then he kissed her with all of the passion and love he had in his heart. As she kissed him back, the first rays of the sun peeked over the ridge shining on them. They ended the kiss and Garrett laid his forehead on Dani's.

"Marriage to me won't be easy, Sweetheart. I have strange hours and I'm gone sometimes days at a time. I never know when I'll get a call. The work I do can be dangerous, but I promise I'll never take unnecessary risks."

Dani laid a finger against Garrett's lips. "I would never ask you to give up the work you love for me. I know your job is risky. I've seen the hours you keep and know firsthand how you can be interrupted at any time." She giggled thinking about how many times it had already happened. "But, I know God is taking care of you, and I trust Him to keep you safe. Thank you for loving Micah as much as I already love Seth, Betty and Lucas. I look forward to being a part of your family." She kissed him and laid her head on his shoulder as they watched the sunrise together.

Epilogue

Labor Day. Dani looked out the window to check the weather. It looked like a beautiful day for the festivities. She dressed, and then helped Betty get the boys ready. Garrett walked in while she prepared breakfast, and they all sat down to have their meal together.

Since Dani was able to help more with Micah, she insisted Betty and Lucas go out of town for a week after the wedding.

Lucas had not told anyone where the couple would go for their honeymoon. But Betty had told Dani she did not care where they went. She looked forward to spending time with him.

The ladies packed the food and necessary items for the Labor Day event. Things for the wedding and the honeymoon had already been taken to the deli. Garrett loaded the rest of the things into Dani's car and waited for the ladies to come out. Seth was especially excited. He was going to be the ring-bearer in the wedding. The ladies got in the car ready to leave.

"Oh, I forgot my bouquet." Betty rushed back into the house, returning with the flowers. "Okay, let the festivities begin!" she gushed, excitement making her almost giddy.

Large crowds were already coming into town. Garrett and his deputies had blocked off the streets at the town square for the booths and arcade rides the night before. Tents were set up and Lucas had two big grills smoking in front of the deli. Garrett parked the car behind the building, and they piled out, each one ready to work.

"Hey Dad, I see Mr. and Mrs. Guthrie. Can I go around with the boys?"

Mike had already told Garrett to send Seth over to them when they arrived. They would watch him while the others worked in the food tent.

———✤———

The clock on the square chimed noon, announcing time to start the serving lines. People picked up their plate and utensils from Betty. Dani gave them a bun and the men put the meat on it. From there, people went on down the row filling their plates as they walked. Long tables for eating were set all around the square. It took close to an hour to get the crowd their meal.

While everybody was seated, the mayor and councilmen took the opportunity to make their speeches. As the men spoke, the five members of the wedding party dressed. Cindy had already taken Micah to join her family for the ceremony. As the speeches were about to end, Reverend Jenkins stepped into the deli to make sure everyone was ready.

The men took their places on the gazebo platform and turned to watch the ladies walk toward them. Dani came out first in a soft pink strapless, tea-length dress. As she walked up the gazebo steps, she glanced at Garrett and winked. He grinned; winking back at her. Then Betty walked out in a beautiful ivory skirt and jacket. She carried the bouquet of red roses.

No one teased Lucas about the tear that escaped his eye as he gazed at the woman he loved. The ceremony was brief, and the pastor told Lucas he could kiss his bride to the applause of the crowd.

Then Reverend Jenkins addressed the audience, "Before we leave to enjoy the rest of the festivities, please indulge us one moment while our good sheriff asks our new early childhood director a question."

Garrett walked over to Dani, while Betty and Lucas stood to one side, arm in arm. He stepped close and looked down at her. "Three days ago you told me you would marry me any time, any place. Did you mean it?"

Dani's hand flew to her mouth. "Garrett, do you mean here, now?"

He nodded his head.

"But we don't have a license." she moaned.

"Right here; it's another perk of being the sheriff." He patted his pocket, grinning at her expression.

She grinned back and took his hand. They walked together to stand in front of the pastor. Betty took back the bouquet Dani held. She and Lucas took their place on either side of Dani and Garrett.

"Folks, it seems we have one more wedding to perform." The reverend looked at the two standing before him and grinned. "Who gives this woman to be wed to this man?" He asked.

Lucas and Betty said, "Her family."

Seth presented the rings to his dad at the appropriate time, whispering to Dani, "I kept the secret real good, didn't I, Mom?"

A tear slipped down Dani's face, as she bent over to kiss his cheek. "You certainly did, my son."

They finished the ceremony and Reverend Jenkins told Garrett he could kiss his bride. The groom gathered Dani in his arms molding her to him. The kiss lasted several seconds, much to the delight of the crowd who whooped and hollered as they clapped.

When Garrett released Dani, she laid her hand along his cheek and told him, "You'll always be my Prince Charming."

Dear Reader,

Thank you for taking the time to read the first book of the Lincks series. I hope you enjoyed reading it as much as I enjoyed creating it.

I started my writing career very late in life. I wrote this first story in July, 2013 just before my sixty-fourth birthday. Starting out with a scene in my head, all I knew was that I wanted the heroine to meet the sheriff after an accident. I sat down and began typing a story that took on a life of its own. I cried with Dani over the loss of her family, felt a little hysterical when Adam took little Micah and laughed as Dani and Garrett discovered their love for each other.

I didn't come to know God until I was thirty-one years old. That day changed my life forever. In 2011, I was diagnosed with Non-Hodgkin's Lymphoma. It sounds crazy but that was one of the best blessings in my life. I drew so much closer to God during that time and I was a far better person at witnessing that I had in the past.

Now, I feel like God has inspired me to write my books. It is more like He is the writer and I am His fingers. If this book touched you in some way, I would love to hear from you. If it made you ask questions, contact me and together we will find answers. You can reach me on my Facebook page or email anytime.

My biggest hope is that it caused you to think about God and His presence in your life as much as it entertained you.

May God bless you!

Carol Clay

Carolclayauthor (facebook)
carolclaywrites@gmail.com

A Fairy Tale Kind of Love

Enjoy this excerpt of

Love's Sweet Sentence

Book Two of the Lincks Series

Carol Clay

Chapter One

"It's just as well they fired me, because I would have quit anyway." Amanda Black paced the living area of her high rise apartment trying to get her temper under control. "After giving that company the best years of my life, they fire me. Six years! And all because I objected to the 'different direction' the new owner wanted to take the magazine. I was the editor! Of course I objected! They changed a wholesome, Christian magazine into one of those smut rags everyone else prints."

Talking out loud was a bad habit, but there was no one who could hear her or who cared if she did. "Problem is, what am I going to do now? I'm twenty-eight years old, and the magazine was the only place I've ever worked."

Like it or not, her last production as editor went to press yesterday. Amanda felt the tears stinging her eyes, but she refused to cry over it anymore.

"I'm through feeling sorry for myself. I have to find something different that renews my passion for life."

Her phone beeped with a text message. "'Sorry about the magazine. Need to see you in Lincks. Have a proposition to discuss with you." Dani Austin had sent the message. Amanda relaxed as she thought about her friend.

The two of them were as close as sisters when Dani had lived in Chicago. After losing her parents, her half-brother and his wife in a span of four months, Danielle McMichaels had adopted her newborn nephew, packed everything she owned and moved her new son to the little town of Lincks, Missouri.

There she fell madly in love with the sheriff and had been happily married for almost a year. Amanda and Dani kept in close contact, but had not seen each other in person since she moved.

Amanda returned her text. "What is this about?"

Dani's reply was, "This has to be discussed in person. Let me know when you are arriving."

She couldn't imagine what the cryptic message meant. But knowing Dani, there would be no further information until Mandy arrived in Lincks.

What was so important in Chicago anyway? She had not taken a vacation in more than three years; there was never time before.

The return text read "See you in one week. This better be good." Amanda pulled up Google Maps on her cell phone to locate Lincks. She never traveled in the United States unless it was flying for business. Any vacations were spent in Europe or resorts on different islands. "It's time I see something besides museums and sand."

Amanda took her car by the shop the next day to make sure it was roadworthy, since she did not drive it more than two or three times a week. Living within a mile of the offices, Mandy usually walked unless the weather was bad or when there were meetings away from the building.

"Can I pick up the car tomorrow?" she asked the shop owner.

He took his time as he looked her over head to toe. "I can have it ready this evening, if you want it delivered personally."

"I'll be by tomorrow to get it." She scowled and walked away before she told the man how she really felt.

The day before she was scheduled to leave, she picked up her dry cleaning and stopped by the post office to have her mail held. After emptying the refrigerator of any perishable food, she pulled her suitcase from the closet and searched through her belongs to decide what items she needed to pack.

Much later she glanced at the clock beside her bed. "Oh, shoot. I was supposed to meet Michael five minutes ago." She changed her outfit and walked to the restaurant down the street.

She knew her date was probably late. *He hasn't worked less than twelve hours a day since I've known him.* As she walked, she wondered how she could tell him she was leaving for a couple of weeks. She did not mention it before because she knew he would be angry. He never did approve of her friendship with Dani. Although he never actually forbade her to see her friend, he made his feelings known. Dani disliked Michael equally as much. She had often told Mandy he was too controlling. Amanda learned over the years to never talk about one with the other.

Mandy thought about her relationship with Michael as she hurried inside the restaurant. Both of them were extremely busy with their professions. It was almost a burden making time for each other. She appreciated the "'understanding" they made when they first began dating. Neither of them objected to the other's last minute cancellation of a date. Michael was usually available to escort her to social functions and as such, she was expected to go with him when he asked. The time or two she had suggested they might see other people, Michael had only laughed. He insisted he was not interested in dating any other person and saw no reason why she should want to either.

She waited until the meal was over to tell him about her trip. "Michael, since I lost my job, I've decided this would be a good time for me to visit Dani. I haven't been able to go since she left and I really do miss her. I told her I would be coming tomorrow," Amanda spoke quietly, hoping he would not make a scene in the restaurant.

He stared at his date, frowning as he pulled his credit card from his wallet. He handed it to the waiter never taking his eyes off of Amanda. "We'll discuss this outside." He knew too many people in the place to say what he planned to tell the woman. Instead he sat back in his chair and waited for the server to return with his card never taking his eyes off of her. He almost chuckled as he watched Amanda brush the imaginary wrinkles from her dress.

As soon as the card was returned, Michael rose and moved to Mandy's side. Taking her elbow, he brought her to her feet. He applied enough pressure making sure she complied. They moved through the restaurant looking like the perfect couple, Amanda with a model's good looks and Michael, the handsome business man in complete control of everything.

It was only after they walked outside of the building and Michael turned Amanda into the alley, did the mask of poise slip from his face. "Why haven't you mentioned this to me before now? I've made plans for us during the next two weeks, and you know full well how I feel about Danielle McMichaels." His fingers tightened on her elbow. "I have a good mind to forbid you going."

Amanda knew he would be angry, but never expected him to react like that. "Michael, you're hurting me. I'm going! I want to see my friend. If you are going to act like this, I think we should stop seeing each other." She was shocked the words actually slipped out of her mouth. She expected she would pay for the mistake.

Michael's hand moved from her arm to her throat wrapping around one side and squeezed. Abruptly, he dropped his arm to his side. "I'm sorry, Amanda. I didn't mean to hurt you. You caught me by surprise. I suppose I can rearrange our plans while you take your little trip. You will be back in two weeks and no longer. When you return, we will plan our wedding. You're not going to spring these little surprises on me again."

"I wasn't intentionally keeping things from you, Michael. I didn't want us to argue about it either. Dani only asked me last week. We haven't seen much of each other since then."

"She better not be trying to talk you into things like she did before she moved away. Personally, I haven't missed her influence on you one bit," he stated.

"I'm sure she's lonely. We've talked often about how much we miss each other. I know she's not your favorite person, but I love her like a sister. I'd like to see her before I look for other work." She wasn't about to mention the proposition Dani had written about.

"Fine. I give you permission to go," Michael seethed as he walked away leaving her standing on the sidewalk. He never told her to be careful or enjoy herself.

Amanda sighed. She knew they didn't love each other, but their relationship was comfortable most of the time. She thought about the time or two they'd discussed their future. Neither of them pushed to make a commitment until now. *Do I want to settle for a marriage to someone I don't love? I'm not sure I even like him at times.* She had all but given up on finding love.

CPSIA information can be obtained
at www.ICGtesting.com
Printed in the USA
FSOW04n0920200416
19382FS

9 780986 233135